The Bloody Medallion

Empty-Grave
Vanilla Edition

by
Richard Jessup

writing as

'Richard Telfair'

Empty-Grave Publishing

Dear Reader,

The Bloody Medallion is a great introduction to Richard Jessup's writing style under his pseudonym—Richard Telfair.

The rest of Jessup's work will be released over time and my intention is to have just about everything he wrote back in print by 2015. Project information and updates are available at www.RichardJessup.com.

And now you best buckle up because Secret Agent Montgomery Nash drives fast and hard—and he doesn't like pulling off at the rest stops.

A.Nicolai
Empty-Grave Publishing

empty-grave.com - website
facebook.com/pages/empty-grave-publishing/114806311932977
- facebook
twitter.com/emptygravepub - twitter
feedback@empty-grave.com - comments, concerns, contact

Contents

Chapter One

ONLY A HANDFUL of men outside of it are familiar with the Department of Counter Intelligence. And that is as it should be, for the D. C. I. is engaged in war—fierce, bloody and hidden—and its secret weapon is secrecy itself.

The field of battle is the entire world. The limited wars, the light engagements, the skirmishes, the hand-to-hand knife fights are fought in the dark streets of Rome, Berlin, London and Paris, and in the dark forests of Germany, the rugged hills of northeastern France, the mountain passes and ice-water streams of northern Italy, and on the dusty plains of Spain. The objective is always the same: Offensive Intelligence.

My name is Montgomery Nash and I am an agent in the European Section, —th Division, Fox Head of a first squad. Most of our work is done in teams. The Department will, on special assignments, send out one man, but usually all pursuits are handled by the basic, two-man tandem that is the first to meet the enemy—and so it is called the first squad. The Division is composed of five such two-man units. Section is the final group and is in charge of a given geographical portion of the globe in which its members have made themselves specialists.

Section plans the overall projection of a pursuit, then sends orders down to Division, which in turn deploys the first squads. No one in my job knows how many Divisions there are in a given GloSec (Global Section) but I have heard there are more than thirty sections that make up the Department of Counter Intelligence—the D.C.I.

Five years ago I was a hotshot lawyer in Cleveland about to marry a long-legged blonde who was finding it more and more difficult to keep her hands off me as the wedding date drew near. I was making fifteen thousand a year. Why would I leave a setup like that to wander into the most ruthless, cold-blooded, brutal and agonizing job on the face of the earth?

I've asked myself that question ten thousand times. I still am not sure that I can answer it. Perhaps way down deep inside of me I know. I'm sure I do. But flag waving and emotional, nationalistic pride somehow always manage to come out corny. I think of myself as much too cynical to admit to any such simple dedication as fighting in my own way for the specific right to be a free man. Yet, in any honest self-examination, it must come down to that. There is no substitute for freedom. And there isn't one of us in the Department who doesn't know how close we have come to losing that precious thing.

Such were my thoughts on a morning that held an autumnal chill and the pungent odor of burning leaves in the air. I lay in bed watching the last of some very dead leaves cling desperately to the branches of a tree. I was bored with London—it's left-hand drive, warm beer, wrong-headed landladies—and I felt a growing desire to go home. I snaked one arm out from underneath the blankets and took the latest letter from my sister and re-read it. The kids were fine. Mother and Dad were okay. Ohio had a good team that year. Harvard had a poor one. It went on like that—newsy, gossipy, and mentioning names that I did not know, and, of late, less and less of those that I did.

Five years. Time goes by with a rush when you are active and away from home. Jo, the long-legged blonde, had married a doctor and had two kids. Dad was about to retire from his job as manager of a Cleveland department store.

Five years. There have been moments on a pursuit when I thought time was very limited and there would be precious few seconds left to me. And there were periods when there was a limitlessness to passing time, and the pursuit became a dull, tedious job that was not worth the effort.

I am past thirty-one now. It would be difficult to return home and start law again. Was it impatience and boredom, or had I really had it? Did I want to tell Division Able Head to go fly a kite with his neat collection of pursuit reports, or did I just want another pursuit that would get me into some live action again? You can concern yourself with some pretty basic problems in the morning while watching a tree cling to her dead little leaves.

Paul Austin, my partner on Fox Head first squad, was in Scotland doing some trout fishing and we still had another week to go on our mission leave. So many days of twenty-four-hour-a-day work gives you accumulated leave that must be taken before you are assigned another pursuit. I had spent most of the last week trying to pin down a redhead I knew in the West End theater district and was thinking that a long ride in the country might turn the trick when the last leaf was torn free of the branch and fluttered to the ground. Now the tree was naked and alone.

The phone rang. "Yeah?" I was expecting it to be the redhead confirming our date that afternoon, but the sharp voice of a trunk-line operator filled the ear piece.

"Trunk call from Firth of Monarath for a Montgomery Nash."

"Who is calling, please?"

"Is this Mr. Nash?"

"Yes."

"One moment sir." There was a series of clicks and then Paul's voice was with me.

"Monty—Monty—are you there?"

"What is it? Run out of trout flies?"

"Listen—Monty, on the last pursuit—the Belgian thing, remember?"

I frowned. The mention of a pursuit, under any circumstances, let alone over a long distance phone line was a solid breach of a classified service. "What about it?" I asked cautiously.

"Put this down and don't miss it. I haven't time."

"What is it!" I insisted.

"Are you taking it down?"

"Yes."

"Coordinates seven seven six four down. Eight, nine ten and eleven across. Map R-sixty two triple A. Got that?"

"Yes—yes—but what the hell is it?"

"I can't say any more. Monty—please—I'm not fishing...."

The line was dead. I jiggled the hook. "Operator. Operator! This is official business. Get that number back please."

"One moment, sir."

I waited. I saw a dark spot on the floor beside my foot and wondered what it was. I stooped down and touched it. Wet. Then I realized that I was sweating and the end of my nose was dripping a steady stream. "Operator! Operator!"

"I'm sorry sir, The party has disconnected."

"Let me talk to your chief operator, please."

"One moment."

A cool, slightly aloof voice came to me. "Chief operator here."

"Do you recognize Code Seven Zero dash four?"

"Yes, sir, I do. One moment please." The voice was sharper now. I almost grinned. The magic number. It was an emergency code that all chief operators knew. In a moment I was talking a Division Able Head. "Rex?"

"Who is this?"

"I haven't got time to explain—Fox Head first squad. Get on these coordinates and line up that brand new IBM cross index you've got. I'm coming right down to explain." I repeated the figures Paul had given me and hung up the phone. I stood still a moment. Paul, I thought, I hope you make it, buddy. I stared at the tree. "You and me will wait until next spring, old dear."

I don't remember dressing. I was deep in the Antwerp pursuit, retracing days and hours and conversations, examining expressions and looks of approval or disapproval, and the million other little things that had gone into setting up a message drop for the Balkan Area with an agent working in the packing plant of a Belgian cheese exporter who had offices in Prague. Whatever the hell was wrong, we would have to get the man out of the Antwerp packing plant. And we would have to warn the Balkan Area to resist all communications that came through Prague.

My mind was struggling for sharp images in a foggy distant plain that was the past three months. The cab wove its way through the Long Heath Road section, caught the double drive west and sped toward Worthington Gardens. Forty minutes after Paul had called, I stepped out of the cab before a neat stone building very much like any other stone building in the area and went up the front steps. Gus was on the door. "Able Head wants you in the lab right away," he said.

I nodded and went down the nearest flight of stairs for two floors into a subbasement. It stretched back into an abandoned bomb shelter that had been closed off on the further end from a street entrance.

Rex met me at the door. "We traced the call. A public phone near a pub called the Tartan Inn. The local constable found Paul dead. Curious."

"What?" I said, feeling pain along my jaw line as I clenched my teeth.

"Paul had been stabbed in the base of the brain with a thistle thorn. They grow them up there, you know. Wild, of course."

I pressed my thumbs against my eyeballs trying to get back into the room and reality. You don't live and think as one for over three years as Paul and I had done without coming to think of the other as part of oneself. I felt his loss in what seemed physical pain.

"Take off your coat." Rex said. I became aware of the lab boys around me. I shucked out of the coat and pulled the tie down. They had a rubber around my arm before I knew what was going on, and then the sharp jab of a needle.

"We're putting you under for a while, Monty," Rex said as they led me back to a chair. "Narcosynthesis. We're going to have to pump you dry—and fast."

"'kay." I said, already feeling the effects of the drug cloud my brain.

Another voice came in then. A cool, calm, quiet voice that I wanted to tell things to. I would tell that voice anything it wanted to know. I would even break down and cry if it didn't ask my most intimate secrets.

"He's under," I heard someone say.

Chapter Two

TEST QUESTIONS first," I heard the voice say. "Are your eyes blue?"

"Yes"

"Do you like the idea that you are a slim young man, not too handsome?"

"No, I would like to be a little taller. Yes, taller and with shoulders like Paul."

"You like Paul, don't you?" The voice was at least ten blocks away and muffled with cheese cloth.

"Yes, I like Paul."

"You were trained with him as a first squad, weren't you?"

"Yes." I said. I felt as comfortable as I would in my mother's lap. I didn't want to ever leave this place and I wanted to tell that voice anything and everything.

"You went through six months of basic training as Marine recruits at Parris Island with Paul, didn't you?"

"Yes. Six Months."

"They were difficult months, weren't they, Monty?"

"Very difficult. Sometimes we cried."

"You and Paul would cry. Why would you do that?"

"Our muscles ached and we couldn't sleep."

"After your Marine training, Monty, what did you do?"

"We went to Washington for further training. Yes, it was Washington. We had a good time in Washington."

"Why did you have a good time?"

"Lots of girls in Washington." I said. "I like girls."

"Did you and Paul ever like same girl?"

"No."

"Did you and Paul ever have an argument?"

"I couldn't tell them that."

"You and Paul had an argument, didn't you?"

"Yes. But we made up later."

"Want to tell me about the argument?"

"Yes, I will tell you about it," I said to the wonderful voice. "It was after we were through with our training in Washington. I was made Fox Head and Paul Fox Tail. He thought he should be Fox Head."

"Did you come to blows?"

"No. We yelled. But we did not fight."

"How long did the yelling go on?"

"A long time. Maybe ten minutes."

"Is that a long time?"

I didn't answer. The light over my head was getting brighter.

"Give him another shot. He's coming out of it."

There was a sharp pain in my arm and then the voice began talking to me again. "Do you like it here?"

"Yes. It's very nice."

"Is ten minutes a long time to yell?"

"Yes. A long time. Paul and I never yelled again."

"Why not?"

"I don't know. I guess it's because we like each other."

"How many pursuits have you been on together?"

"Eleven."

"Ever save Paul's life?"

"Yes. Three times."

"Tell me about saving Paul's life."

"We were in Austria on leave. I pulled him out of a river. That was the first time."

"That was very brave of you."

"Paul would have done the same thing for me."

"Tell me about the other times."

"Once on a pursuit in Algiers I shot a—a woman in the back as she was about to shoot Paul."

"Did it bother you to shoot a woman in the back?"

"Yes. We got drunk for a long time after that."

"And the third time that you saved Paul's life?"

"The third time?"

"Yes, Monty, you said you saved his life three times. You have only told me about two of those times. Don't you want tell me about the third time?" the voice asked.

Did I? I wanted to tell him everything. But somehow I couldn't.

"Tell me, Monty, how you saved Paul's life the third time," the voice insisted.

"On a pursuit—"

"You were on a pursuit, yes, go on—"

"We were trapped in a building in—" I stopped. Where was the place? "Trapped in a building in—"

"Is it important that you know where you were trapped?"

"Yes, it's important."

"Then try and think. Was it Berlin?"

"No."

"Paris?"

"No, it wasn't Paris,"

"A satellite country?"

"Yes—yes—it was a satellite country. It was—Czechoslovakia—and we were leaving and Paul wanted to—"

"What did Paul want to do?"

"He wanted to stay and try and help a local agent. Check—"

"The agent was a Czech and Paul wanted to help him."

"Yes."

"But you didn't."

"It was too much of a risk. The pursuit was in jeopardy."

"And in this delay—you saved Paul's life."

"Yes."

"How? Tell me how?"

"We were running for a car—and they came after us. They were shooting. Paul fell and I went to help him. He had turned his foot and couldn't walk for a moment. I stayed with him and we shot at them—and then Paul was able to walk again and we escaped."

There was a long pause. I thought the voice had gone away and then I felt the sharp jab of the needle again. In a moment the voice was back.

"Monty, we believe that Paul has defected."

"Paul—Paul defected? I don't think—Paul would do that."

"We know that he has, Monty. We have proof."

"Proof?"

"Monty, we know that Paul has defected."

"No. Paul would never do that. Not Paul. Not Paul."

"Yes, Monty, Paul has gone over to the other side. Isn't that terrible?"

"Yes, it's horrible."

"And the information he phoned to you from Scotland was false and misleading. Did you know that?"

"False—information— Paul's information not true. I don't believe that."

"Do you remember the coordinates he gave you?"

"Yes. I remember."

"Can you repeat them?"

"Yes. Do you want me to repeat them?"

"No. But a good agent like you, Monty, knows that there hasn't been an R-map in use for over eighteen months. What do you think of that?"

"I don't know. I don't know."

"Paul gave you information about coordinates that are no longer in use."

"Paul did that?"

"Yes. Paul is a traitor."

"Traitor?"

"Poor Paul is a traitor. Isn't Paul wicked to become a defector and a traitor?"

"Wicked. Yes. Paul is wicked."

"Paul is also wicked enough to have an affair with the wife of the Belgian cheese exporter, isn't he?"

"Yes. He had an affair with Helga. He is wicked."

"Did you know that Helga was a D.P. that came from Poland and had lived in the East Zone of Germany before she met the cheese man?"

"No I did not know that."

"Did you know that Paul was not fishing in Scotland, but secretly having an affair with Helga?"

"No, I did not know that."

"Are you sure you didn't know he was with her?"

"Oh, yes, I am sure. Paul is wicked."

"Would you suspect Helga and Paul?"

"I don't know."

"Would you suspect Helga and Paul?"

"I don't know."

"Would you tell me the name of the contact Paul had with Helga while you were on a pursuit in Antwerp?"

"Contact?"

"You know that Helga and Paul were double agents, don't you?"

"No, I did not know that. But Paul is wicked."

"What is the contact's name and how is he approached?"

"I don't know."

"Think, Monty, you don't want to be wicked like Paul, Helga and all other traitors, do you?"

"Oh, no."

"What is the contact's name and how is he approached?"

"I don't know—I don't know—I don't—"

The light over my head seemed to be getting brighter again, and I waited for the sharp jab in my arm, but it never came. The light got brighter and then suddenly it died out. The last thing I heard that wonderful voice say was: "He's asleep now. Maybe as much as four or five hours before the stuff wears off."

Chapter Three

I WAS STILL in the lab and I had a hell of a headache. I opened my eyes and tried to hide from the light. Gus Sample and Tris Guardian were there beside me, and Rex. There was another man that I didn't know. "Gimme an aspirin." I managed.

"Drink this," Rex said. He handed me a glass of milky liquid and I downed it, fought to keep it down and then sank back in the chair.

"Here." Gus shoved a cigarette in my lips and I puffed on it hard. I stared at them.

"Did you get anything?" I asked.

"Enough," Rex said. "We know where to start."

"Paul?"

"I told you, dead."

"No questions?" I asked.

"No question about it. Glasgow Division confirmed it. He was still wearing his chemical I.D. tags. One spot of acid on the back and his name came up. It's Paul. And he's very dead."

I puffed on the cigarette while they looked at me and I thought back to the first time I met him. A big-shouldered football player fresh off the All-American football fields with a mind like a steel trap. I'd go to the gates of hell with Paul Austin, and now he was dead.

"What gives?"

"What was Paul's relationship with Helga de Loon, Monty?"

"He was sleeping with her."

"No love?"

"Not that I know of."

"Those coordinates he gave you. Are you sure you got the right map classification?"

"I don't miss." I said. "Try me."

"Okay—okay. You got them right." Rex took a few steps around the edge of the nearest lab table. "Now, did Paul say anything else? Did he add anything beside the map references?"

"Yeah. He said he wasn't fishing."

"Any idea what he meant by that?"

"No idea at all." I paused. "On the outside, just shooting in the dark, maybe he meant the map reference wasn't just kidding around and the remark could mean he really had something."

"What do you think it might be?" Rex asked with the oily smoothness of a well-honed knife blade.

"I don't know. You pumped me with the narco-stuff." And then I remembered the voice telling me that Paul had been a defector, a traitor. "Look here, Rex, what about this defection business."

"What about it, Monty?"

"Is it true?"

"You tell us."

"Are you kidding!" I asked. "What the hell kind of remark is that?"

"I can't tell you, Monty."

I hesitated, feeling the hair on the back of my neck begin to stiffen. "Okay," I said as casually as I could, "security. Meantime, how about a cup of coffee before I lose the breakfast I didn't have."

Rex laughed, and we all left the lab and went up into the house. I washed my face in ice-cold water and drank three cups of coffee. Tris Guardian and Gus Sample launched into a long narrative about a blonde and a week end, with Rex and the stranger joining in their laughter. But they really didn't laugh. And they didn't take their eyes off me for a second. One of them was continually watching me. It was done smoothly and you wouldn't have guessed it in a hundred years if you hadn't done the same thing yourself.

We ate kippers, cheese and had more coffee. They continued to laugh and talk that foolish way to cover their watching and I let my mind drift back to Paul.

He was always running off somewhere between pursuits to do something that required a great deal of physical effort and was, to my mind, of questionable fun. He climbed the Swiss mountains, and he hiked Wales and Ireland, he biked around Spain; he hunted, he fished and he chased girls. I went with him once — several years before — on a bike trip along the Cornish Coasts to Lands End and ended up with blisters in the most unlikely places and drenched to the skin after pedaling through three days of constant cloudy drip. We spent another two days in the most Godforsaken inn with the worst food in the world before giving up completely and taking the train back to London. Paul, on the other hand, seemed to thrive on such endurance feats and though we were as close as a first squad, our activities of relaxation went separate ways. This trout-fishing trip had been of a comparatively mild nature compared to some of his other ideas of vacationing, and I remember wondering if he had begun to ease up a little.

In our association as agents in a first squad I had come to know Paul Austin as I knew no one else. There are things that can take place between two human beings that are impossible to put down on an IBM card and watch fly through the metal warrens and come up with a neatly charted behavior projection. The voice of a man when he says he will cover you in a tight corner will send another into the mouth of a cannon because he has heard the whisper of a dedicated man, a man willing to sacrifice his life to do what he has said he would do — cover you. The look of a man when he is depending on *you* can telegraph the meaning of that man much more accurately than the psycho-graphs and the nodding, knowing pronouncements of the limited view of a behavior analysis by a psychologist.

I knew what Rex was doing. I knew the stranger was observing me critically. They believed, and possibly had information to support that belief, that Paul had defected. But they wouldn't lie about his being dead. So I was the only link they had between what they believed about Paul and a situation that had the Division Able Head in a stew.

The talk and the forced laughter continued. That went on for another half hour before I turned to Rex.

"What gives?"

"Don't you know?" He looked at me with surprise.

"Don't know nothin'," I said.

"We're waiting for a check on those coordinates you say Paul gave you."

"You sound as though you didn't believe me," I said, and could not keep the tension out of my voice.

"We don't."

There. He said it. And in a way I was relieved. "What is it you don't believe?"

"Let me put it this way," the stranger said. "We know how close a first squad can be. You and Paul were one of the best first squads in European GloSec. With Paul's activity, we must naturally be suspect of every pursuit you and Paul have been on."

"Who are you?" I demanded.

"That is unimportant," the stranger said loftily.

"I agree with you," I turned to Rex. "Are you putting a formal charge against me?"

"We haven't decided."

"Suspended, at any rate."

He was slow in answering, "Don't be bullheaded about him," he said, nodding his head toward the stranger. "You know we're a team organization. He's part of the team. He wouldn't be here if I didn't think—if Section didn't think—he was an important part of the operation of European GloSec."

"You didn't answer my question, Rex. Am I suspended?"

"Yes," he said finally.

"Are you going to place a formal charge against me?"

"We may. It depends on what we come up with in the cross-examination of the R-map coordinates."

"But after that, Rex, what happens?"

"If we can prove that you and Paul were acting in collusion and that in fact, you also were a party to his defection, you will be placed under arrest, returned to the States for a Department hearing, a hearing before all Sections Leaders. They then will decide about pressing charges against you for the violation of the National Security Act."

"And you expect to get all that out of the R-map coordinates I gave you?" I asked.

"We can begin there. We've already begun."

"My record doesn't mean a thing, I guess." I said, trying desperately to keep the strain and emotion out of my voice. I saw the stranger lean forward slightly. He wasn't going to miss this. He would remember the slight hesitation in my voice and the creeping emotion. That was going to go down against me. I almost sneered at his smug face.

Suddenly I knew how an enemy agent must feel when picked up. When I awoke this morning, I was a successful, respected member of a very private and secret organization. Now I was reduced to defending every act and every idea I had had since joining the D.C.I. and that had made me feel, I thought, what I feel. They were suddenly all "the enemy," because they were attacking my person. From behind the fog of my own indignation at being suspected, at having them tell me that my closest and most trusted friend was a double agent, I began to see how I must have appeared and how I must have been—confident, with undivided loyalty and some measure of confidence that it was the other fellow that fell into the traps, but never me."

"Your record," Rex said, "is suspect."

"All of it?"

"Every line of reports you've made since becoming a Class One security agent, Fox Head first squad, is being examined right this minute."

"Along with Paul's."

"With Paul's."

"Then you're going to get something, Rex," I said, "if for no other reason than we operated as the Department trained us to do—as one thinking person. What ever Paul has done, or is supposed to have done, will be reflected in my own reports because of that. Why not take them individually?"

"We prefer to do it this way."

"Why?"

"Because everything you've ever done in this Department has been done in partnership with Paul Austin. That was the way the record was made, that's the way it's going to be examined. At least on this level. What Section Hearing Board will do back home is none of my affair."

"Will you tell me something?"

"What?"

"When did you learn of Paul's supposed defection and double agent activity?"

"I can't tell you that." Rex replied.

"What can you tell me?" I asked. "Doesn't it mean anything that I submitted to narco-stuff—"

"You didn't submit. We had that needle in your arm the moment you walked into the lab," Rex replied.

"I'll take a lie detector test."

"Unreliable," the stranger interjected at once.

"Who says!" I demanded hotly. "Listen, Rex, you too, Tris, Gus—you strap me into a detector and ask me any question you want. Anything."

"I can't do that, Monty. Sorry." Rex replied. There was a knock on the door. Rex got up to answer it. I got up and started to move with him. Tris and Gus stood with me and watched me carefully.

"Sit down, Monty." Rex said, turning from the door, holding it open. I saw the stats clerk waiting with a folder in his hand. My folder. The one that would spell out lies about me—and I was willing to bet—about Paul. I began to see, in a flash of blood-red rebellion, how the human mind can grow so complex and dependent on machines and graphs and charted cycles that the human, spiritual and emotional elements can be slide-ruled right out of existence.

"Sit down, Monty!" Rex barked. I saw Tris and Gus move toward me, and I saw Rex reach out for the folder.

I nodded and slumped my shoulders a little. Tris and Gus moved in quickly on either side of me and reached for my arms. I stepped in tight against Tris Guardian and had his .45 in my hand before he knew what had happened. I rammed it in his guts. "Don't move!" I said. "Come inside, sonny." I said to the clerk.

"Don't be a damn fool, Monty!" Rex said tensely.

"Come in and close the door." I said to the clerk. The young man stepped inside, his eyes wide with fear, and closed the door. I pushed Tris back hard, and he bounced off the edge of the table. The dirty dishes and coffee cups fell to the floor.

"Give me the folder." I said.

The clerk started to move forward, extending the folder, when Rex stepped in between us. I did not hesitate. I moved in and dropped Division Able Head with a short, hard left-hook into the stomach. I held the .45 up and showed it to Tris and Gus. "Now, boy," I said, "give me the folder."

He handed it over. I removed the half-dozen type-written sheets and shoved them into my pocket. Rex was helped to his feet by the clerk, and I saw him trying to control his heaving stomach.

"You can't get out of here, Monty." Tris said. "You know it's impossible to get in or out unless it's okay."

"Put it—down, Monty." Rex gasped.

"Come here, sonny." I said to the clerk. "And move slowly."

The boy looked wildly at Rex and then moved toward me. "I'm taking him with me. I want out and, while I probably won't have the guts to kill him, I'll beat his face to a pulp, Rex, if you try and stop me."

The stranger piped up at that moment. It was almost a hysterical shriek. "He can't look at those papers!"

"You want to try and take them away from him, Mr. Allison?" Tris Guardian said.

"Out of the door and straight to the front, sonny," I said to the clerk. "Better not do anything, Rex, until you get a call from him."

"You won't hurt me, will you, Mr. Nash?" the clerk asked fearfully.

"If I do, it's because they'll force me to."

The boy looked at Rex. "Please—Mr.—"

"Go ahead, Monty. We won't do a thing. I give you my word."

"I wouldn't take it, Rex. Somehow, it doesn't mean anything any more." I pulled the clerk around in front of me and worked my way to the door. We were outside in the hall when the boy closed the door after him.

"When are you going to let me go, Mr. Nash?"

"About that time, kid," I said and hurried him down the stairs to the front door.

"What time, sir?"

"You figure it out." We were outside on the street. Rex had a little MG that he loved to tinker with and that I knew would do a flat one thirty-five. I pushed the boy in beside me, threw a glance back at the door and jerked the gears. We shot down the street and three minutes later were on the double East drive heading back for the heart of London.

Chapter Four

THE SIX PAGES were spread before me in a West End pub. They spelled out in simple deductive reasoning, that was in turn spelled out in simple words, two facts that would nail me and Paul to the cross if I didn't know that at least one half—my half—of the report was not true.

Fact one concerned itself with Paul's associations and lusty sexual weekends with Helga at a small tourist park off by itself and perched on a dune overlooking the Hook of Holland. The deduction offered in the report was that Paul's girl-chasing activity had been an actual behavioristic pattern seized upon to act as a cover for the meetings and information exchanges between Helga, and/or other agents. There was no doubt in the deduction of the report that Helga was a red agent.

Fact two was my part of the long-supposed activity of double-agent-ing by my frequent and unusually long periods of time spent in various museums in five countries during the course of our pursuits. The longest period of time noted spent in any single such institution was while on the Belgian pursuit. This was reasoned to be a patterned approach I used for information and other exchanges with enemy agents. My interest in art was dismissed as not being "likely" considering my middle class background, formal education and practically negative exposure to painting as a child, discounting any later intense interest. Nothing, the report stated, in my background supported the logic of such undue interest as I had shown in painting and works of art.

The report went on like that, a machine-made character to replace the one I had lived with all my life. An IBM personality to bring me into "proper focus and perspective." The deeper I read into the report, the closer I came to the mad idea that it was all some kind of a joke that Rex, Paul, Tris and Gus had worked out to needle me. I talked a lot about painting and spent a lot of time trying to paint. I took an awful ribbing about my efforts, too, and this would indeed be a wonderful gag.

But a gag would not include information about Helga and Paul. It would not include narcosynthesis.

Back to the report. I read it again. I had to accept Rex's statement that Paul was dead. That would not be much of a gag. Paul was dead. He was on to something. And Rex claimed he was a traitor and a defector, and had been one for some time. Did Rex suspect Paul before I had called him about the coordinates? "No," I said aloud to myself. "The R-map reference put him on it. And maybe there was something in Paul's personal reports that had mentioned Helga. It would have been routine for Rex to make a check of Helga since Paul had been sleeping with her. And there was the possibility that Helga's background could have brought up something with a red herring tied to its tail.

All right, Nash, I thought. Have another warm beer and settle in with trying to plot it out. I got up and moved through the swirl of cigarette smoke and loud talk in the pub as the early dinner crowd and the white-collar workers pressed the bar.

I went back to my table with other thoughts than those of the report and the defection of Paul. I was struck with the measure of loneliness that can envelope a man when it is forced on him. I am not a party-goer. I don't dislike crowds, but I prefer it quiet, that's all. I am not bombast and cheers, but I don't mind it in others. I lived alone and saw a few friends I had made in London and in Liverpool, once in a while taking ten days in Paris, or two weeks in Rome, but for the most part I liked drives in the country with my red-headed friend in the West End theater, Martinis before dinner, and talk. On rare occasions, a dinner party with friends. I lived that way by choice. It seemed to me a good balance between the crazy harebrained schemes of the D.C.I. pursuits.

This loneliness that would not let me call my red-head or see my friends, that herded me into the shadows and the back corners of pubs, though much the life I lived while on a pursuit, was not of my own choosing. The life during a pursuit was a choice, as was my life at home. Here I felt the heaviness of the outcast, of the man alone. I collected myself, shoved the papers into my pocket and emerged from the pub into the cold, rainy London night. I slouched through the streets wondering about the machines that had created a new man by the name of Montgomery Nash. Certainly in the eyes of Rex and my friends at Division, I was no longer the Monty Nash they had known. I was someone else. A man with the same name, but with the important difference that I was not to be trusted.

I could not go see the redhead, nor any of my friends. Rex would have them staked out, and I wouldn't stand a chance. The logical place for me to turn, I thought, would be to Paul. But Paul was dead.

I found myself walking around Oxford Circus, pushing and being pushed by the late crowds and the straggling employees of the expensive shops. It had to begin with Paul Austin—Paul Austin and Helga.

***

I worked my way east out of greater London as far as the buses would take me and caught a taxi. I was short on money, but the fifty odd pounds I had would be enough at the moment.

It is roughly fifty miles from the outskirts of London to Ramsgate. The ride was quick and the driver knew the roads. He tried to talk, but I cut him off. I wanted time to think. I wanted time to figure out what Rex would put into operation, what I would do if I were in his shoes.

It was close to ten and still raining when I paid the driver. I stood in the darkened streets and gazed out toward the sea, my mind and my body aching with fatigue. My arm was sore from the narco needles, and I wanted a cigarette. I had the cigarettes, but no matches.

I began to walk. Ramsgate had been plastered by the Nazis in 1940. It's one of the first towns of any size on the way up to London approaching from the continent. The fly boys would get nervous and drop their loads at the first sign of flak and turn tail for home. They did a pretty good job and would have done a lot more damage if it hadn't been for the caves in the cliffs.

The harbor is good, and there is a narrow entrance from the sea. Two long stone piers run out into the harbor and one of them is a promenade for the afternoon strollers. I saw dimly, and only because I knew they would be there, the reflected hulls of the yachts winking up at me as I worked my way out on the pier. I knew exactly what I would need. Keeping my eyes open against the rain was getting difficult when I spotted the right size. It was a little fishing boat that looked new and would probably have a good engine. It was anchored to a buoy off the pier some hundred yards and the approach to it was covered by a neat little group of cats, yawls, jacks and lug sailors. I walked to the water's edge and slipped into the cold water without a sound. I stroked underwater just keeping my head up, not bothering to turn around to see if anyone was watching me. I was reasonably sure I had slipped out onto the pier unnoticed.

I had to wait for my strength to return before I was able to pull myself up over the side of the boat. I cracked the window of the cabin and reached inside for the latch, opened the door and stepped inside.

27

It was warm inside the little boat. I stumbled around until I found the engine housing, lifted it up and felt the block. It had been used that day, probably within the last three or four hours. I breathed easier. She was warm and that would make it easier to start.

I stripped off my raincoat, jacket and shoes and then turned to search the cabin. I found a flashlight in the second drawer I tried and guarded the beam. It was a clean, bright cabin that looked well cared for. I turned my attention to jumping the ignition, and, when that was accomplished, I turned to watch the automatic gauges and breathed a sigh of relief. It was nearly three quarters full of gas and, from the looks of the over-sized engine, could probably make it to the continent easily, considering it was a fishing boat and therefore geared for economy.

The one thing that I had hoped for was with me and I slipped out of the cabin and forward to slip the buoy line. The boat was caught in the tide and began to drift backward into the channel. I remained huddled in the stern pushing off other boats as well as I could, until we were well away from the piers.

Cautiously, I pressed the starter button. There was a loud cough—once—twice—three times—and then she kicked over and settled down into a smooth, low, vibrating hum. I pulled the wheel around, set the clutch and moved out toward the sea. In a half hour I was clear of the coast with no sign of anyone following me. In an hour and a half I was alone in the straits of Dover, running without lights and heading due east for the Belgian coast north of Ostend."

The rain continued for the next five hours. I did not see another ship, or any lights. I stripped down to the skin, rummaged around in the cabin and pulled on a scale-covered pair of trousers and a foul-smelling sweater, putting my own clothes over the hood of the engine.

It is roughly eighty miles from Ramsgate to the strip of coast where I wanted to land above Ostend and I was batting away past the lights of that city at a little before four in the morning. It would be close, but I was sure I could make it before dawn. I opened up the throttle and the engine that was designed for power rather than speed labored heavily. I left the Ostend lights behind and began moving in closer to the coast. I had another half-hour before dawn, and, though I was not sure I was at the point along the coast where I remembered a barren strip of beach, I could not wait for daylight. I turned the head toward the beach, strapped the wheel and began to dress in my half-dry clothes.

The sandy beach grated against the keel and the boat stopped. I cut the engine and remained still. Silence.

I moved to the bow and crouched down low. I could make out the sand dunes and the reaches of grazing land beyond the dike. I dropped in to the sand and dashed for the cover of the dike, remained still for a full three minutes and then got up and climbed to the top.

He was an old man dressed in fishing clothes. He stared at me. "You beached your boat deliberately. I saw you!" He shouted.

His French was that bastardization the Belgians speak in the rural areas. "I'm sick—" I said in French. "Help me—sick—"

I staggered toward him. He approached me suspiciously. I stumbled a few feet away from him and he reached out instinctively to keep me from falling. I hated to do it, but it was clean. I caught him in the back of the neck with a hard hand chop and he folded up in my arms like a sack of wet sugar. I pulled him into the protection of the dike and went through his pockets. He didn't have much money, but it was enough to get me into Antwerp where I could then exchange an English pound without too much suspicion."

"I shoved the several thousand Belgian francs into my pocket and hurried across the fields toward a little house and the road beyond it. To the southeast I knew was Brugge. I could get the local train to Ghent, and there I could change for the Paris-Antwerp Express.

I would have just enough time to get cleaned up and ready to walk into Helga de Loon's house the moment her husband left for his office. Paul had described with great glee once how perfectly he had timed de Loon's leaving for the office with his own entrance. "I'm sitting in the old boy's chair, Monty, before his tea cup is cold!"

I thought about this, my teeth chattering against the cold channel winds as I walked toward the road that would take me to Brugge. Paul had even told me where the key to the rear garden gate was hidden.

A pair of lights stabbed at me out of the darkness a few moments after I had started up the road. I dropped down to the side behind a bunch of low grass and waited. The heavily-loaded truck pulled up alongside and for a moment I thought it was going to stop. But it kept on rolling, I dashed after it and grabbed the tailgate. I pulled myself up and caught my breath. I bounced through the awakening Belgian countryside.

Chapter Five

THE SUCCESS of an agent depends on two complementing factors. One is important as the other and they are fifty per cent of success. An unexceptional appearance and adaptability—these two factors shroud the agent most effectively. Let the agent have an unusual characteristic and he will eventually be caught. He must move as those he mingles with. He must sound like them, he must behave as they behave. Let him make one single error in judgment about the price of an ice cream cone and someone will look at him with suspicion. And suspicion is the undoing of the intelligence agent."

Antwerp is a big, roaring, ambitious, hard-working metropolitan city. It boasts a highly sophisticated citizenry. It speaks two languages by nature and from birth, Belgian and French. It moves like most of the big continental cities, from early dawn until late at night with a heady, brawling progress. You can lose yourself easily in a city like Antwerp, and if you are an agent working against the time when you will be caught by your own people as well as the other side, you want to get lost as soon as possible. I did this, first by going to a working quarter near the docks and buying—with the old man's Belgian francs—clothes that were not English. I changed in a public toilet. I gave my old clothes to a dirty-faced little boy and told him I was a friend of his father's and that he was expecting them. Then I moved back to the cafés near the railroad station at the head of the main street and began to change the pounds into Belgian francs with the waiters.

The only thing I kept was my acid ID tag around my neck and the .45 I had taken from Tris.

It was time to call on Helga de Loon.

The house was a fine white one made of brick. I walked around the side of it, as Paul had described, slouching along with my head down, taking the exaggeratedly long steps that Europeans get from walking great distances, and found the key as Paul had said.

I waited. I looked at my watch. De Loon was supposed to leave at nine sharp. I had about five minutes. I peeked through the iron gate into the gardens, and was a little startled to see both of them sitting at a table just inside the glass-walled room that looked out over the gardens.

I saw him put his paper to one side, get up after folding his napkin carefully, then rolling it tightly and putting it into a silver ring. He kissed Helga. She smiled and said something to him and went back to reading her share of the paper. A touching domestic scene.

I forced myself to count to an even hundred before I unlocked the gate and stepped inside. I was inside the glass door before she knew I was there. "Hello, Helga," I said.

She looked up, her mouth open. She was beautiful, with her blue eyes, the long blonde hair that trailed way down her back, and her wide, red mouth. She wore a thin nightgown with red rose buds at the top and a filmy, much thinner dressing gown on top of that. I could see the rosettes of her breasts and the dark shadow that dipped mysteriously from the hard, white little belly. "My God!" she said. She dropped the newspaper. "Monty!"

"Don't scream, Helga. Don't move. Don't do anything. Is there a maid? Paul said there was a maid named Katrin."

"She's—she's in the kitchen."

"Will she come out here again?"

"Not unless I call her."

"I want to know about—you and Paul," I said.

She looked at me, her blue eyes opening up a little more and then something happened. Her face hardened. The relaxed face of the confident, secure housewife who had kissed her husband off to the office disappeared.

"What do you want to know, Monty?" She asked coolly. I think I really began to suspect her right then. It was the wrong thing to say. She was too cool. She did not once turn in fear to see if her husband had forgotten something, or if the maid, Katrin, would suddenly appear on hearing voices. It would be different with Paul, the expected lover. She would have everything arranged. Now she was hard. Very hard and she was ready to play hard games.

"Were you in Scotland with Paul?"

"Scotland?" She repeated herself. "Scotland?"

"With Paul. For the past week."

"I haven't been out of Antwerp."

"Can you prove that?"

"I don't see that I have to."

"Paul's dead, Helga. He was murdered—yesterday morning."

It didn't faze her. It didn't even mean enough to lift an eyebrow. "Poor Paul," she said. "Anything else?"

"What happened up on the Hook, Helga?"

She blushed. Even the toughest of them get caught when you bring up their love affair. "I don't see that it's any of your business."

"One word from me to de Loon, Helga, and you will be out on your head."

She thought about that a long time. "What do you want?"

"Yes, my dear Monty, what do you want, and what are you doing in my house? Helga, how dare you. Get dressed!"

Gautier de Loon waddled into the room, his round face trembling and quivering as he walked. He was a big, absolutely bald man, tall and thick. His belly extended before him in a mountain of flesh, all of it garbed in the shiny black of the Belgian business man's uniform of wool serge.

"Gilly, darling—" She stood.

He moved past her to confront me with the grace of a battleship. "What is the meaning of this!" He demanded.

At the door I saw the maid, a hard-eyed tough-jawed woman, watching the scene. I wondered fleetingly if Helga had managed to signal the maid, who in turn brought de Loon back—or had she sent for him on her own on seeing me there? I decided Helga had not done anything. She was too frightened to have called the big man back.

"Hello, Monsieur de Loon. I hope that you will not make a terrible mistake and assume that I—"

"I assume nothing! You are here! And she is undressed!" De Loon shouted. He stabbed a fat finger at his wife. This was not anything new. Old de Loon had had his suspicions before this.

"Gilly, Monty was looking for you," she pleaded. "You must believe me. Oh, what have I done to you, poor darling, to make you so insanely jealous!" She tried to go to him, but he wasn't having any. "Gilly—please."

"Go put some clothes on at once!"

She dabbed tearfully at the corner of one eye and in so doing covered her look at me. She turned and fled from the room.

De Loon was still crowding me. And he was a boy that could crowd. "How did you get in here?" He demanded.

I nodded toward the garden. "Paul—you remember—Paul—my partner—of course you do," I said, and moved away from him. "He told me where to find the key, when you would be leaving the house and—ah—other details."

He was livid. His belly began to tremble and his fat head waggled, his jowls fluttering. "You devil! Both of you! Devils! Out—out—Get out of my house!" He advanced toward me and I moved toward the glass door. "I ought to—to—have the police on you, you swine."

Suddenly it struck me that it was all much too theatrical. Helga had fled on cue, after de Loon had appeared almost too perfectly. And then they played their scene out with gestures, by-gosh and by-damn.

He was still raging at me when I saw the maid disappear behind a curtain. I stuck around doggedly. He followed me into the garden, his voice and the color in his face rising. And the more he yelled, the more stubbornly the idea clung to me that it was all staged and phony.

There was only one thing to do to find out. And I had to talk to Helga. I pulled out the .45. "Shut up, you fat slob!" I said and rammed the barrel of the gun a full eight inches into his gut. He stuttered to a stop, looked down at the gun and then up at me. "Turn around and let's go back into her room—and not a word, fatty, or I'll rip that blubber off of you by the layer and feed it to the cat."

He turned without a sound and waddled back into the house. "Her room, quick!" I said in a whisper.

He marched ahead of me into the hall and turned to his right. A door opened and the maid appeared. Beyond her I could see Helga busy with a phone. I stepped aside from de Loon and flagged the .45 in the maid's face. She nodded her head, turned around and started back into the room.

Helga looked up. She caught on in a second and dropped the phone into the cradle. She stood. She was framed against the light of her window and the outline of her body was clear through the transparent cloth of her gowns. I moved quickly and snatched up the phone. What I had hoped for had happened—the line was still open. A voice was calling loudly. "Helga—Helga—what ess it! What ees going on, dere! Tell me!"

The line went dead.

I flagged the operator and kept my eyes on both of them as Helga moved around to join de Loon and the maid.

"*Oui, monsieur?*"

"Was that a long distance call just placed?" I hesitated. "I would like to know the charges."

"One moment, please."

I glared at them. "Don't move, de Loon. I'll put one in your head fast."

"You are acting very foolish, Monty," Helga said. "What do you think you're doing?"

"Monsieur, the call was to Paris. You will be charged the minimum, four thousand francs."

"What number was it please?"

"One moment, monsieur."

De Loon glanced at Helga. And then suddenly, without any signal that I could see, they rushed me.

The women dove for my face and de Loon tried to grab the gun. I squeezed one off and watched him drop to the floor like a wounded elephant. He didn't even twitch. There wasn't a drop of blood, but he was very dead. I held on to the phone and kicked the maid hard with my right foot and slammed her back across the room. She came up with a wicked-looking pair of scissors.

I was fighting Helga off now, using my elbow, but she was getting at my face. I chopped her down with the .45 and then turned just as the maid lunged at me with the scissors. I didn't want to shoot her. I hated like hell to do it. So I just let her have a fast one between the eyes and watched her slam back into the same place across the room.

The operator was saying something in my ear. "What number— what was that, please?" I managed to say.

"Is there anything wrong, monsieur!" There was alarm in her voice.

"My sons. Twins. Their birthday and there's a party—" I said.

She laughed and I could hear her sigh of relief. "Here is the Paris number, monsieur. Vosges 8-5980."

"Thank you, mademoiselle." I said and dropped the phone into the cradle.

I stepped over the body of de Loon and hurried through to the front of the house. I peered through the door to the street. There was one man walking by, but he was very old and did not appear to have noticed the shots. I went back to the gardens and walked to the gate. The lane was empty. I went back into the house and into the bedroom.

They were just as I had left them. The maid, I knew, had been dead before she hit the floor. I touched Helga's temple and felt her pulse. I guessed she would be out for another hour and slipped the gun back into my pocket.

I turned to face the room. Working with the kind of quickness that is sure and doesn't miss a thing, I tore the house apart and found nothing except money, all kinds of money—dollars, French, Belgian and Swiss francs, lire, pesos and West and East German marks. I found de Loon's passport and the *carte identité* of the maid, who was a Danish citizen named Sara Annders. But I did not find a single thing that would put Helga in a time, a place with perhaps another name.

There were jewels, several large diamond rings and a curious-looking gold medallion on a gold chain. I stuffed the largest of the rings into my pockets along with the Belgian and Swiss francs, which was not only the largest amount there, but also happened to be the most stable currency in Europe. Then I turned to examine the medallion.

I placed it flat in the palm of my hand and twisted, hard. It unscrewed in my hand. Three pieces of faded red cloth fluttered to the rug. Just red cloth. There was nothing else inside.

I put the cloth back in the medallion and screwed it down tight. I dropped it into the jewelry box and turned to Helga.

It was not easy to get her to come out of it. She would have a hell of a headache and she might even have to go to the hospital, but she would be able to talk to me. I finally had to dump a pitcher of cold water over her to shock her out of it. The filmy gowns stuck to her body like tissue paper. I could see clearly everything that Paul had found so interesting. And no wonder.

She groaned and moaned a little. Her eyes opened and she saw de Loon and the maid. She stifled a scream and looked at me with horror in her eyes.

"Do we talk now, or do I have to put you down beside them?" I asked.

She started to cry, and then she broke into hysterical laughter.

I let her go on like that until it worked itself out into a case of dry, heaving sobs and she was more or less quiet.

"Listen to me, Helga. I know you come from Poland, and that your name probably isn't Helga, but something else. I know that you lived in the German East Zone before you slipped across into the West Zone. I know that your interest in Paul was strictly for laughs, but Paul was that kind of a guy, an easy mark for a woman who wanted to have fun."

She had just about stopped her sobs, but she kept her head bowed and she didn't look at de Loon any more. "There are several ways you can play this, Helga. You probably know by now that I'm not a businessman. Businessmen, regardless of what the propaganda says, do not shoot their competition. My only interest now is Paul."

She lit a cigarette. I continued, moving over to pour myself a cup of coffee only to find it was tea. I drank it anyway, with four spoons of sugar. "You don't have a passport—most people who slip across the borders out of East Germany and the other countries don't. On the other hand, you could have been slipped across."

She didn't move.

"Trade is a wonderful thing. De Loon, the fat bastard, probably made a deal with them that would run something like this. Marry Helga So-and-So, let her operate from behind the respectability of your good name and office, and we'll let you have export to the Balkans. It was big money, so Fatty went for it. What the hell did he care what the Americans gained or lost? It was every man for himself.

"All right, Helga Whatever-your-name-is, you're a respectable housewife of a respectable Belgian businessman. You begin to operate. And one by one the friends that de Loon brings home make themselves known to you, that is, they pass along information. And other than that you're just Mrs. de Loon. You collect the information, have it shipped out through the cheese shipments along with whatever else they might need, say in the way of industrial diamonds, fine machine dies, and anything that cant be crammed into a diplomatic pouch or that might be suspect in a packing case at a border checkpoint. But who is going to go punching holes in cheese? Nobody, Helga, nobody. It was a beautiful setup, and we recognized it and planted one of our own men in your organization—"

She spun around and looked at me.

"Oh, he's all finished now. Did his job and got out. That's what Paul and I were doing here. We got him the job. *You* got him the job, Helga, by giving information to Paul unaware. Our man applied and got the job, with the help of our inside information."

I did not hesitate to tell her about the man in the cheese shipping plant. Rex would have yanked him out of there half an hour after the suspicion coming in on Paul had rubbed off on me. She was getting nervous now. She was smoking a little faster.

"Now, Helga, the point I want to make is this: What are they going to think or do, sweets, when I drop them a line and tell them that we have a plant in their Antwerp drop, as well as in Prague? They're going to come looking for you, sweets, because I'll tell them you did it." I grinned. And it was the first time in such a long time that it felt good, but strange. She had a look on her face that was more than just fear, it was horror.

"Monty—"

"Oh, I'm not finished yet, Helga. I want to know whose idea it was to pump Paul, how you tumbled to us, when you did tumble to us, and what the operation is they've set up against us."

"I don't know what you're talking about."

"Wake up, Helga," I said. "If they don't get you it'll be because I've broken your neck. Paul, sweets, is my best friend. Somewhere, when he was with you, he went wrong. *I want to know about it!*"

I moved toward her. At that moment I could have easily broken her neck and slung her beside Fatty. But she was as afraid as I was determined, and she broke first. She backed away.

She moved to the jewelry box. I moved with her. She scooped up a handful and offered it to me. "Take these—and I'll give you money."

"Are you kidding?" I watched her closely.

"They will kill me. Please, Monty, let me get away to South America. I promise you, once I'm out of Europe, I'll do anything you say—" Her free hand slipped over the medallion and palmed it with an ease that would have made a Mississippi river-boat gambler green with envy. "Take them, Monty—"

"Sure," I said and stepped forward. I grabbed her arm and wrenched it. The medallion dropped to the floor. I picked it up. "This cinches it, baby."

She sank to the floor as if there wasn't a bone in her body.

I flipped the gold coin. "You don't have any choice, sweets." I said. "How does the story go? A secret society composed of members of a tank squadron that fought at Stalingrad. Most of them were young kids. Students. You would be about the right age, Helga, to have been an ex-student fighting the war."

She began to moan.

"Let's see, how does the story go? The squadron was trapped by the Nazis. It was a particularly tough outfit and you had raised hell with the panzers so the Nazis were good and sore at you, but finally it was surrounded and you surrendered to them. That night, half-ordered, half-demanded by the Nazi soldiers, the squadron was divided in half and one half was marched into the area between the lines of combat. The rest of the surrendered squadron was rescued when the opposing Russian forces were so outraged they swam through freezing rivers and took chances with their gear on the thin ice, some of it caving through and going to the bottom. But enough of them got across the river to swarm over the Nazi position and destroy it. The rescued members of the tank squadron dipped their battle standard into the blood of each machine-gunned comrade and swore blood oaths against the fascist, regardless of what flag he claimed or what language he spoke."

I unscrewed the medallion. "I heard that story from reliable sources, Helga, and always doubted it. But not any more." I dropped the red and faded cloth before her. "The blood dipped battle standard, Helga. And the oath you took bound you to fight the only real friends the Russian people ever had."

"Your country!" She spat it out with contempt.

"And a hell of a lot more countries beside mine."

She seemed to gather strength from somewhere. Perhaps it was the bits of cloth before her and the memory of that terrible day when the Nazis had cut her friends down mercilessly. Perhaps, on the other hand, it was none of these thoughts, but a hardness and a zealot's conviction of his cause, or it could have been just fear. Of me, of them, of life. Whatever the reason or the source of her strength, she stood up and wiped away the tears on her cheeks and turned to face me. She held out her hand for the medallion and I handed it to her. She placed the bits of cloth back inside and screwed it down tight. "What's the use of going over the past, and the reasons for what we do?" She asked. "Yes, I was there. I saw it happen with my own eyes. And it was me that went from corpse to corpse and let the standard soak up their blood." She turned to face me. I still had not figured out where she got her strength. "There were nineteen of us, twelve men and seven women, none of us over twenty. Others heard of our oath and wanted to join. We let them, because—" she shrugged— "many had sisters and brothers that had died that day."

"We did nothing at first. We held no meetings, and we saw little of each other when the war was over. Then this medallion was sent to me and to others. It was accompanied by a letter from one of the nineteen. It swore us to secrecy and reminded us of the oath we took and the bloody rag was inside for each of us to see and to make us remember. The fascist, the letter said, was all that stood in the way of socialist progress."

She laughed cynically and glanced down at de Loon and the maid. "What we didn't know was that they had learned about the oath we had taken, we remaining members of that squadron, and sought to use it to their advantage. The fight, they said, was not only in the battle-fields where the tanks were deployed and the infantry marched, but everywhere socialism was not first in the hearts of the people."

She looked up at me. "There are hundreds who carry the medallion now. Each with a faded bit of red cloth that is supposed to be the dried, brown blood of those who were killed by the Germans that day near Stalingrad. It has gone beyond the moment when the soul cries out for revenge, Monty. Even the Secret Police do not know who we are. No one knows who the leader is, who gives the orders, who the reports go to, but we all know, because there are only three of us left of the original nineteen who swore the oath, that to disobey, to fail in a mission, means death."

She stopped. "Well, Monty, super-American spy, what do you think about that story?"

"I believe it." I said, meaning it. There are times when you believe because you must. And this was one of those times for me. This woman was not lying. She was not afraid. She seemed to be at the end of something. But what ever it was, I believed her.

"Then you were sent here?"

She nodded. "Just as you guessed. To set up an information drop and courier station." She looked at de Loon. "They bought him—with money."

"And the maid?"

She sneered. "A provincial communist. A useful tool."

"What about Paul, Helga?" I asked.

She had moved to a desk and was looking inside what looked to be a cigarette box. I realized too late she was not looking for a cigarette. She had some closer than that. She held up the capsule, smiled, and then popped it into her mouth. She bit hard, then grimaced and swallowed quickly. It was over before I reached her.

She fell sideways into my arms, the pain tearing at her.

"Helga, please—please—Helga, tell me. Was Paul—a defector—"

She tried to speak. She moved her lips. I put my head down close to her mouth and then she jerked so violently that I could not hold her. She fell to the floor, kicked out against the pain and then lay still.

I pried the medallion out of her hand. I stood. The causes of death are ten thousand. The wicked are supposed to die hard. They are just as dead regardless of how it's supposed to come.

Perhaps Helga de Loon or whatever her real name was, died wickedly and without confession. But she did not have to confirm my story of suppositions about her and de Loon. She did not have to tell me of the medallion organization, and I believe she would have told me the truth about Paul Austin. So it was Helga that I thought about when I slipped out of the house and into the morning garden and away from the stillness of death. I did not think about the useful tool, or the mercenary exporter. I thought about Paul and Helga together and I wondered what they might have thought and felt deep below the surface of the continual lies, double-cross and theft that was the trademark of the spy.

I did not leave the garden right away. It was not that I was afraid to leave. I lingered while the sun came up bright and hard and there was noise in the streets and the distant roar of a world Helga had somehow missed knowing.

Chapter Six

I CROSSED THE BORDER into France near Dinant and caught a bus in Givet that took me to Reims. A local train from Reims put me in Paris after midnight. I went immediately to a telephone—Vosges 8-5980 did not answer.

It began to rain and I caught a cab. "Café Alié, Malakoff." I said to the driver. Malakoff was a suburb of Paris that I knew well from a pursuit, one of the first that I had worked on with Paul. Café Alié was where we had spent a great deal of our time.

We rode the avenues and boulevards in silence. The rain was thick enough to keep the driver on his toes, but after settling into the seat I forgot about the rain and let my mind drift back to Helga. I rubbed the gold medallion, fingered it and finally pulled it out of my pocket to hold in the palm of my hand. Something was disturbing my thoughts that had nothing to do with Helga or what had happened back in Antwerp, or anything that had happened earlier with Rex. I kept rubbing the medallion trying to find the thing that was—somehow—missing and it was not until I had paid off the cab and was entering the Café Alié that it struck me. Paul was the disturbing factor.

Not Paul's possible defection, or his death, but his absence. I missed talking it out with him. I missed anticipating a meeting with him and the low, tense voice that we would use when we began to compare notes, if any, and decide what the next step should be, how we should approach it and all of the other angles that we had been taught to examine when on a pursuit.

And I caught myself thinking of Paul as being a right arm that will itch at the elbow even though it has been amputated.

"Monsieur!" André came from behind his place at the cashier's desk, hand out to greet me.

"*Mon ami*," I said and forced myself to smile. We shook hands and I could see his wise old eyes looking at the door behind me. "Paul's not here." I said.

He hesitated a split second and I could see the question forming on his lips, then he clamped his mouth shut. I don't think he had ever believed our story about being ex G.I.'s going to school in Paris when, two years earlier, he had let us sit for seven weeks waiting for a contact. "You are soaked to the skin. Come, cognac for you at once!" He turned and called to the waiter. "*Pierre! Cognac, pour le monsieur. Vite!*"

I sat in a well-worn chair beside his high stool at the cashier's desk, the chair of honor in the Café Alié, and was grateful for the cognac. I drank it in a gulp."

"*Sucore le cognac!*" He demanded of the waiter, then turned to beam upon me, his round face forever moist and his dark eyes seldom serious. But I saw they were serious now. His face was a mass of wrinkles smiling down at me from his height, but his eyes were wary.

"So, monsieur, you are alone, eh! What is it? *Cherchez la femme*?" He laughed at his own joke. "Has he forsaken you for a woman?"

"He's dead," I said.

There. He has suspected. He had known. The wise old bastard.

"But how, monsieur?" He crossed himself quickly and offered a blessing.

"Murdered, André. Cold-blooded murder."

"*Sacré Bleu! No!*"

"Yes." I accepted the second cognac, a huge triple shot in a water glass, the sight of which made André grunt with satisfaction as if giving his approval to a man-sized drink. I thanked the waiter.

"How did such a thing happen?"

"I cannot talk of it." I said.

"No. I should not have asked," he replied. I drank the cognac and felt it rush to my head. I stood. "I need a place to sleep—only until you close, *mon ami*," I said. "Then I have to leave."

"Does your being here—your sleeping and then running, does it have to do with the murder of Monsieur Paul?"

"It does."

He nodded. "Ah. *Oui*. You two were that close. You would be looking for his murderer." He heaved his bulk from the high stool and waddled through the café to the back. He opened a door. We were inside his living quarters.

The two rooms were furnished with turn-of-the-century, cheap, factory-made French furniture. It is the worst-looking furniture in the world. The light was dim. A huge chair by a radio was mute evidence of quiet hours he spent alone in back of his café. André lived alone. His wife had been killed during the war.

I sank wearily onto the couch. He protested. "No—no, *mon ami*. You must sleep in the bed!"

It was in vain. I was too tired to care. "Promise me you will awaken me when you close the café?"

"Must it be so?"

"It must be."

"I will awaken you. Sleep, *mon vieux*," he said and turned out the light, closed the door behind him and left me to the silent world of my thoughts and the death that lay just off a garden in Antwerp. And of the death that lay in the morgue in some lonely Scottish town.

The cognac behaved as it was supposed to. I was asleep in seconds. It must have been seconds because it seemed only an instant since my fat friend had left me to when he was there again, shaking me awake.

"Monsieur—Monsieur—Monty!" André spoke loudly.

I crawled out of the deep, hungry for sleep. I nodded. "*Oui*—I'm awake." I stood. André had coffee ready. And another man-sized shot of cognac.

André wanted to talk, but my silence soon dampened his enthusiasm for bringing up old times. He excused himself and went into his room. I heard the bed sag under his bulk and, in a few moments, before I had finished my second cup of coffee, he was snoring.

I picked up the phone and tried Vosges 8-5980 again. I don't know exactly what I was expecting, but certainly not what happened.

"Duval, *oui*?"

"Monsieur—" I said, stalling for time. I wanted to hear the voice again.

"*Oui*—what ess it?"

It was the same voice I had heard when I snatched the phone from Helga in Antwerp. "Monsieur Duval," I said.

"*Oui*—*Oui*—who ees there?"

"A friend." I said. "A friend in desperate need."

"What is your name, friend?" He said cautiously, but with interest.

"Many of us do not have names. We carry the medallion."

I held my breath. It had been a chance, but it was the only way I could bring him out. He could hang up, in which case it would take me two day through contacts to find out the registration and street address of Vosges 8-5980.

"I don't know what you are talking about, monsieur. I'm afraid you must be joking me—*oui*, joking."

There was a hook into him now. If he really didn't know anything about the medallion, he would have hung up. I glanced at my watch. Quarter past three in the morning. Anyone other than someone who knew—and understood—what the medallion meant, would have cursed me and hung up.

But he hadn't. He was playing it cute. I played right along with him. "You go ahead and think of it as a joke, monsieur, and there may be no time for apologies."

"I don't understand what you are talking about."

"I hold a medallion, Monsieur Duval. I need help."

"Help—"

"Monsieur!" I said desperately. "I would let certain parties know that you refused to help me. I would do that, monsieur, if you do not stop this silly game. Who is there to hear what I say on the telephone? Who would be listening, you fool! I carry the medallion. Is it common knowledge? Is it! Answer me!"

I was trembling. I was playing it wide open and knew it. If the man on the other end of the line was responsible, if he was a half-way clever, intuitive agent, he would know that I was pulling a bluff. There must be a code word for the holders of the medallion. And obviously that was what he was waiting for. And obviously I had not said it.

But I was working on one small advantage. I knew that the organization was so secret that, from Helga's picture of it, it was not likely that many medallion carriers would know many others. And the advantage carried weight remembering Helga's words ... "to disobey, to fail in a mission, means death ..." But if Duval had been a party to Helga's activities, did he also know that she carried a medallion? Had Helga been sending in a distress signal to the man

I had on the other end of the wire for her own sake, or to protect the position of de Loon and the setup in Antwerp.

The it hit me. Duval did know about the medallions. The dead silence ringing in my ear answered me. He knew. And what I had said to him had gone home.

"How can I be sure—" Duval was desperate now.

I had him.

"You can't be, monsieur." I said as harshly as I could. "Where is your discipline, you fool! You must test me."

"But—"

"Listen to me very closely, monsieur," I said, trying as hard as I could to put menace in my voice. "I already know that you are unstable. This conversation with you proves that. Regardless of what you do, it will make little difference. I will make my report."

I hung up.

It was dirty pool. But then who doesn't play it that way when it's a thing called Life that hangs in the balance. I let him stew a little while. I drank another cup of coffee and washed my face. I slipped into André's room and found his closet. His raincoat fit me like a blanket, but when it was belted it was not so bad. I pulled on his beret. I had no cigarettes left and went into the darkened café and took several packages from the case near André's stool. I passed the cognac bottle, snagged it and went back into the room.

I called Duval again.

"Monsieur," I said at once, my voice still carrying the menace I had contrived before, "by now you have thought about it. You have a plan to test me. Tell me of your plan."

Attack! Attack! Get on the offense and you win the day! The training words endured to the point of exhaustion came back to me. It was working this time. It had not always worked. But it was working this most important time.

He spoke. "You carry the medallion. For what reason?"

I answered instantly. "To fight fascism in all countries regardless of flag or the language of the enemy."

He liked that. I distinctly heard him grunt his approval. "What is your name?"

"None of your business." I replied. "Give me your test."

"Are you on a mission?"

"None of your business."

"Where you told to contact me?"

"None of your business. The plan, monsieur. The test!"

There was a long pause. Finally he spoke. "Go to the Rue de l'Iénterieur—number seexty-two."

"Yes."

"Wait there."

He hung up. I dropped the phone in the cradle and stood. André was still snoring. I put money on the table for the cognac, cigarettes and his coat and beret. Perhaps he would be offended when he found it. But the café was not large. He did not do much business. And I felt it was but small return for his great kindness.

I went out the bathroom window. There was no sense in inviting a collaring by any hard-handed Paris cop who might see me leaving the darkened Café Alié.

It was still raining. I hurried down the street several blocks and caught a taxi on the Boulevard St. Cécile and from there rode back to the heart of the City of Light, now dark with rain.

***

Number 62 Rue de l'Intérieur was situated in a dead-end alley. I had expected it. On either side of the darkened opening the ancient houses protruded above the clearing below. I was not about to walk inside. I remained on the sidewalk, hugging the wall of the nearest of the buildings and waited.

A half hour. Nothing happened. Another fifteen minutes. Nothing.

The rain faltered fretfully and stopped. It was getting close to the hour of dawn, but the sky was still black. Another fifteen minutes. And then the truck pulled out of a street to my right, slowed beside the curb and stopped. The lights were put out. I loosened the belt of André's coat and put my hand on the .45. I moved my head instinctively. I wondered what had made me do it and then realized that I was signaling for Paul to cover the opposite side of the alley. That threw me. And I had to bite down hard on my lip to keep from moving.

Someone got out of the truck and moved to the back. I heard the click of the back door opening and closing. The figure re-entered the truck again.

I spotted her the instant she turned the corner in the opposite direction from the truck. She was thin and tall, wearing a black leather coat that hung below her knees. Her beret was pulled down deep, covering her hair.

There was something wrong. She wasn't a whore. She couldn't be out at that time of the morning on a legitimate errand. I knew this because something was wrong.

Then it struck me. The rain had not slicked up the leather coat. She had either just left a house or she could have just gotten out of a car or truck parked around the corner.

She weaved down the sidewalk drunkenly. I steadied myself against the wall.

"Pardon, monsieur—"

I reached out and grabbed her by the belt, jerking hard, and pulled her up against me. I let her feel the pressure of the .45.

"Don't move," I said. "Don't scream."

"Monsieur!" She looked up into my face. The lights snapped on. The truck ground into gear, began to roll. In the light I got a look at her. She was not just pretty. She was beautiful. A kind of perfect-featured face that is so simple, yet so startling when you see it. She did not resist. She had a lot of confidence.

The truck rolled down the curb slowly, pinning us against the wall. I watched the door, waiting. I wanted the truck to come even with me and then I was going to play them out. Then we were all going to get into the truck and talk. That was the way I had it planned.

The truck stopped. It sounded its horn. Once. Lightly. Barely audible in the silence. And then they came from around back of the truck. Two of them. Low and fast. And bigger than any dogs I had ever seen.

The girl jerked back and spoke to them gently. "Take him prisoner."

I jerked at the .45. But I was not ready for the dogs. I had been watching the truck for someone to lunge out after me from the cab.

They did get out of the truck and they came out fast. And I did get the .45 out and up, but the two German shepherds were well trained. One went for the gun hand, the other went for my throat.

We went down, but I managed to squeeze off one shot. I heard someone groan and then I stopped resisting. You don't fight two hundred pounds of fury, one on your arm and the other at your throat. I lay on the sidewalk, face up, both panting faces and long tongues standing over me, on guard.

They came out of the truck. Four of them. They attended the girl. It was she that had gotten my slug. I watched them. I watched the little guy with the square-looking hat come forward.

"You insisted on the test, monsieur," Duval said. He stooped quickly and shot the needle in my arm. I dared not move. The dogs would have torn me apart.

"Take him," Duval said, standing up. I remember they called the dogs off. I remember one of them was taking the girl around the corner, holding her close, as one would do to a badly wounded person.

Then I was thrown into the back of the truck. The dark inside the body of the truck was equal to the dark clouding down on top of my brain. Then they merged.

Chapter Seven

I WAS IN THE WOODS. It was daylight and the sun was on the horizon, cutting a perfect shadow into a mountain. I did not know whether it was rising or setting.

In a moment I found out. The sun dropped behind the mountain and the night rode swiftly down on me. I had been listening for some minutes, preparing to move, to test my arms and legs to see if I was tied, when I heard voices speaking in French.

"I won't do it!" The woman said.

There was a vicious slap. The woman began to cry.

"You will!" A man's voice insisted.

"No!" She was slapped again. Go ahead, do it, I thought. Anything is better than getting slapped around.

She didn't want to do something. He wanted her to. He slapped her, but she still didn't want to do it. Then I heard water being poured into a glass. This was strange. But it was clear. Water was being poured into a glass, or a bowl.

"Get a grip on yourself, mademoiselle." Duval said.

Then I got it. They were going to fix her wound. She gasped. I could hear her sucking in her breath, and then the half-moaning half-shuddering of someone enduring great pain. There were a few quick soft words for her and another of command, guttural, and in a voice that I thought I recognized, but was not sure.

They were concentrating on her. They were not thinking about me. I began to test my arms. It was absolutely dark by now. There was no light near me, only a huge pressure lantern that illuminated their work on her.

I moved. It was a great effort. My hands were not tied, nor my legs. This shook me for a moment. I had violated every reasonable course of action a *good* agent should take. I had willingly—and well—put myself into the hands of the enemy.

Now the enemy chose not to tie me. I raised up and felt around the ground. I was on a thick pile of leaves, damp and a little soggy.

49

I still wore the coat I had taken from André. I reached for the chain around my neck and found the dog tag in place. Everything was as before, except that my right arm was sore from the needle and the .45 was missing.

I sat still and watched a group of half a dozen stand around the table where the woman was seated, stripped to the waist. One man worked on her shoulder while the others offered advice and assistance. I was in something over my head, perhaps the same thing that Paul had gotten into. It was going beyond the single purpose of clearing my good name and of clearing the name of the man who had been my closest friend.

There was a gentle footfall behind me. I tensed, ready to roll with the blow. But no blow came. Instead a heavy boot stopped in front of me and the stock of an automatic rifle was dropped beside the boot. A man stooped before me. He wore a stocking cap and a leather jacket. He held something in his hand. "Cigarette?"

"*Merci.*" He lit it for me. He did not look at my face as he held the match, but turned and watched the work under the light. "She is a brave woman."

"*Oui,*" I said. I settled back. If he was casual with me it would be better if I behaved the same way. I noticed that he was not holding the rifle very tightly.

"What happened?"

He shrugged. "They brought you here with her."

"Duval?" I asked, forcing my voice to be casual.

"*Oui.* You were unconscious and she had been wounded. Shot." He lugged the automatic rifle to his shoulder and stood. "I should be asking you what happened."

"I don't remember." I grinned and rubbed the back of my neck.

"I must get back to my post," he mumbled and disappeared into the woods behind me.

It was time to move now. One way or the other, it was time to do something. While I spoke to the guard I had rubbed feeling back into my arm and it was now hurting enough to know that it would function. I stood up slowly, silently, keeping my eyes on the table. They were still working over her. She was biting her lower lip and two men on either

50

side were holding her arms. They did not see me as I worked my way past them to what looked like a gamekeeper's cottage. I slipped inside the door and saw Duval move suddenly into the darkness.

The room was softly lighted. The man seated at the table looked up and then very slowly picked up a Luger. He pointed it at me. "Sit down, monsieur," he said politely. "You must be hungry and thirsty." He shoved cheese, bread and a bottle of wine across the table at me. "How are they doing with the girl?"

"If they don't put her into shock, she might live," I said. I reached for the bottle and the cheese. It occurred to me that I had not eaten in a long time."

He was big, very big, with a big nose and shaggy eyebrows. He ate a piece of cheese, carving it off in thin slivers with a wicked-looking knife. He put the Luger down on the table, but close enough to grab if I made a move.

"Why did you shoot her?" he asked easily. "It was senseless. The dogs had you down. If she had not been in control of herself after the shot, monsieur, if she had less heart, she might have let the dogs kill you." He shrugged and shook his head. "It was very stupid and —" He shrugged again.

"It was an accident," I lied.

"Of course."

"Where is Duval?" I asked.

"He will be back soon with someone who will question you, monsieur." He smiled. "You should eat well. Very well. It may be your last if the questions, monsieur, are not answered exactly right. Exactly right!" He wriggled his head. "Or pouf!"

I ate. And while I ate I studied the room. There was a window to my right and another across the one room we were in. A door to the left and right, probably leading to other rooms. There were no other guns except the Luger.

He watched me. And I watched him.

***

All of them including the woman, came in after an hour. She was wearing her left arm in a sling, and her face showed the signs of her pain. The men were dark, roughly dressed and quiet. They all carried guns. They came in and settled themselves around the room and began to tear at the cheese and bread and to drink wine. They stared at me. I stared back. The girl went into one of the side rooms and closed the door. I saw now that she wasn't more than twenty. And even in her pain, with her dead white skin, I could not get over the physical beauty of her face. Her hair was dark and had a blue tinge to it. Her face was stark, her eyes blue and deep, and her lips red and full. The men were very solicitous, going to the door of the room and speaking to her.

No one approached me. And then suddenly, there might have been a signal or a gesture that I did not see, all of them moved back out of the house, leaving me alone with the man and the Luger. A moment later a car drove up, the motor racing, then dying.

"Soon now, monsieur," The man said, standing up. He seemed a little nervous. He motioned me to my feet with the Luger and nodded toward the door where the woman had entered.

"There are men with automatic firearms, monsieur. They are all around us. They will kill you instantly—for two reasons." He nodded again toward the door. "Her—and because you have not answered the questions."

"There are no cowards," I said, "Behind a loaded gun."

"*Oui.*" He almost laughed. But the Luger did not waver. I entered the room and he slammed the door behind me.

The room was dark and it took me a moment to get used to the pitch blackness inside. Then I heard the low mean growl of an animal. There was the pad of feet. She had the dogs with her.

"Mademoiselle?" I said softly.

"*Oui?*"

"The dogs—"

"They will not harm you, monsieur." Her voice was thin. "Koko—Rouge! Enough!"

The animals padded away from me. I could hear them sigh and flop to the floor.

"*Merci,*" I said. Slowly the light from outside the cottage filtered into the room, and I could make out its contents. There was a bed, upon which the woman was stretched out. There was a chair beside the window, and the two dogs lay on the floor near the bed. They watched me alertly.

"Sit, monsieur. It will be some time before they come in to question you."

"*Merci*, mademoiselle." I walked gingerly toward the chair and sat down. The dogs swung their heads around with me. Their round, amber eyes shone in the dim light.

"Are you badly hurt?" I asked.

"Not badly, monsieur. Anton called it a flesh wound. He said the women in the Italian underground suffered much more and did not make as much noise as I did." I thought I heard her give a little laugh.

"Anton—was he with you here in Paris—was he one of the ones on the truck?"

"We are not in Paris, monsieur," she said. I heard her rise up in bed. The dogs stood, wagging their tails, but not moving their eyes from me. She swung her feet over the side of the bed. "Give me a cigarette," she said. "And there is a lamp beside the chair. On the floor to your right."

I did not move. She understood my hesitation. "They will not bother you, unless you make a move toward me or the door, or unless I speak to them. They are very well trained."

"I remember," I said. I tossed her the cigarettes and found the lantern. It was another pressure type like the one outside. I pumped it up and lit it. The room burst into a white hot glare from the flame.

She looked at me. She sat perfectly still. Thin—hardly any meat on her bones at all. She smiled and her teeth were a little uneven, but white. She wore a pair of tight-fitting black ski pants and a heavy sweater that had been cut away at the shoulder. The white bandage looked homemade.

In the next few minutes, I studied one of the most beautiful women in the world. She was absolutely exquisite—there was no flaw that I could see. I had never seen such sheer simple beauty in a woman's face. Her manner added to it. She slumped over, making herself round shouldered, and swung her long thin arm up and out as she smoked, dangling her legs.

"If we are not in Paris, mademoiselle, where are we?"

53

She took a long drag on the cigarette and exhaled slowly. Her arm dropped to her lap. "Do you know Italy? Along the French border?"

"Yes."

"A village west of Cuneo. We are near that village."

"*Oui.*"

"Do you carry the medallion, mademoiselle?" I asked.

"I cannot answer you. Not until you have been questioned."

"I understand," I said. I shifted my position in the chair. I could hear the others talking outside. "I am sorry about your shoulder."

"It hurt."

"I am sorry."

"I believe you."

"Truly I am, mademoiselle. I have never shot a woman before," I lied, remembering the woman in Algiers whom I had shot in the back.

"But men, *oui?*"

"Yes. I have shot men."

"So have I," she said simply. "Seven."

"I have killed many more than seven."

"I did not like it. But one must do as directed—" She stopped. "We must not talk any more."

"I understand," I said. "Not until the questions."

"*Oui.*"

"I am sorry, truly, about shooting you and causing you pain."

"I believe you, monsieur."

She lay back down on the bed, and I could see her trying to roll over. She managed it with a sigh. The dogs hopped up on the bed beside her and stretched out, one at the head, the other at the foot. I could see now that one was a littler larger than the other. He would be the male. One Red, one Koko.

"Come, Rouge," I said softly. Both dogs picked up their ears.

"They will not move from my side, monsieur," the woman said in a muffled voice.

I smoked another cigarette and waited. I did not wait long. The man with the Luger came to the door, opened it softly and beckoned me out, putting his finger to his lips and indicating I was not to disturb the woman.

I stood, watching the dogs, and walked out of the room. It was a strange sensation to escape from an evil I considered less deadly than a determined-looking gentleman holding a Luger pointed at my heart. But I had met the dogs. I knew what they could do. I was not sure about the man with the Luger."

I had expected a new face, the face of the one who had come up in the car. But there was just Duval and the others. They waved me to a seat. The guard that had offered me the cigarette held the automatic rifle aimed at my head. This was going to be rough. Yes sir, I said to myself. This is bigger than clearing your name, isn't it?

Duval, in the light, was a man with a small face, shoulders and hands. He had the blackest, most piercing eyes I had ever seen. They moved in around me. There would be no sympathy here.

"What is your name?" Duval asked in the kind of precise French that gives a man away quicker than if he had an accent.

"Montgomery Nash," I said.

"That is your cover name. What is your real name?" He asked.

"None of your business."

"That will get you nowhere, monsieur," he said. The man with the Luger leaned over and spoke into Duval's ear. Duval nodded.

"We know certain things about you."

"What?"

"That—" He hesitated and shrugged his shoulders. "For instance, you are an American."

"I never denied it."

"What would an American be doing holding a medallion?"

I looked up at the man who had operated on the girl. She had called him Anton. "What would a man from the Italian underground named Anton be doing holding a medallion?"

That shook them.

Duval's voice came out of his mouth in a tiny squeal. "How did you know that?" He demanded.

"I know a lot of things."

"Are you on a mission?"

"None of your business," I said. They didn't like that. And they weren't going to stand for it much longer. I waited a moment and then nodded slowly. "I was on a mission. I called because I was instructed to call."

"You called me on instructions," Duval said, "yet you did not know *certain* expressions—"

"Spanish Gold", I Said, saying the first thing that came into my mind. They looked at me. "*Oui*, monsieur, Spanish Gold. See, it means something—but *what* does it mean, monsieur?"

"You are being clever, monsieur Nash," Duval said.

"Not at all. I am only trying to point out, monsieur, that there are cells—"

"What cell?" Duval said at once. The others stirred. I had said something in some way significant and they jumped on it. I seized the advantage.

"I have not asked you, monsieur, what of your cell!" I said harshly. "Nor any of these!" I waved to the standing, waiting men. "Who are you to question me? But let me warn you, monsieur Duval and monsieur Anton—and the rest of you. Consider very carefully before you make a decision."

The man with the luger and several others gathered around Duval. Anton spoke. They disagreed. I tried to hear what they were saying, but the man with the automatic rifle held me back in the chair. Anton slammed his hands on the desk and kept repeating one word over and over. "...*Fini!*...*Fini!*..."

Several others looked at me and turned back to Duval. One of them repeated the same word "*Fini!*"

Duval stood. He scowled at me. *"Un moment,"* he said to Anton. He walked around the table and stood before me. The others waited. Duval rocked back on his heels. "Monsieur, you say you are on a mission, you mention a meaningless expression—Spanish Gold—you mention cells. You seem to know, and yet, monsieur, you know nothing. But, if you are truly what you say you are, then you will certainly know this answer. I will ask you one question."

"Ask it," I said. This was the payoff. I could feel sweat crawling down my back.

"There are only two people who would know my telephone number. Name them. Name them, monsieur, and tell me who it was that gave you the number Vosges 8-5980?"

"Helga—before she died."

The men murmured. Duval studied my face. "Before she died!"

"She killed herself. And de Loon was murdered by an American agent named Paul Austin. I had been working with Austin. That is the reason for my American identity and the American pistol. I have been on special mission to penetrate the intelligence of the Americans. This was done. I became a partner with this Paul Austin. Helga and I worked closely together. Somehow this Austin became suspicious. I learned of his suspicions and returned to Antwerp to warn Helga. I was too late. She had swallowed a capsule such as we all carry. I went through her house and destroyed as many papers as I could and robbed the safe to make it look like theft and murder. Before she died, Helga told me of your phone number—and that she had been talking to you the minute Paul Austin had arrived."

They listened to my story wide-eyed. I had no way of knowing if they were buying it. Paul had been accused by Rex, and all elements supporting Paul's possible defection had pointed toward me as being an aid. If Paul had defected, then I was well within my reason to put the blame on him, and shift identities. Paul would become the enemy agent and I would become the defector.

Duval turned to Anton and the man with the Luger. "It is true," he said slowly. "There was an interruption the last time I spoke with Helga."

"On discovering that Paul Austin had become suspicious of myself and Helga, there was no time for me to contact anyone through normal channels. I had to run. I went immediately to Helga and found her near death. She had taken her capsule and was not yet dead. She whispered your phone number, telling me to contact you." I raced on quickly, not giving them time to think.

"Where is your capsule monsieur?" Anton demanded.

"I gave it to Helga. She was in great pain. Somehow the poison had not acted quickly. I administered the *coup de grâce*." I looked at them heatedly—and then directly at Duval. "Would you have done less for Helga, monsieur?" I demanded.

He did not answer. I was winning. But I was not yet the winner. I pressed the advantage, slightly, just a touch, just a hair to see whether I was over the hump or not. "I came to you, Monsieur Duval, not contacting my regular superior for fear that this American Austin had in some way learned of it. Perhaps that was not wise. But you do not shoot a man for being unwise under such conditions. I contacted you. Spanish Gold is the certain expression of—" I hesitated— "my cell. But because of your admirable but exaggerated thoroughness, monsieur, the pursuit of Paul Austin and whatever knowledge he may have of us, has so far failed!"

"Wait," Duval said.

He motioned to the others to follow him outside. The man with the automatic rifle did not move, but he did offer me a drink of wine. The tension was easing. But I knew they were going outside to make their decision.

They were gone an hour. In that time the girl came out, followed by her dogs. She drank a glass of wine and talked to the guard. Neither of them spoke to me. They stopped talking when the others entered the cottage for the third time.

Chapter Eight

A TOUGH SERGEANT in the Marines once told me that the best way to jump a man was headlong. You have a smaller target and you have the weight of your body acting as a projectile. The chances of being shot in mid air are but ten to one.

Try hitting something thrown at you. I have tried. And I have missed eight out of ten times. I looked at the rifle and the dogs. The car had driven away, and the men were coming back for a third time. If they came in with the wrong decision, it was going to be me and the dogs and the automatic rifle.

They said nothing. Duval smiled and motioned with his head to the one called Anton. Anton came forward and gave me the .45.

"Thanks," I said. And without looking I slipped the clip out and felt for the shells. I shot one into the chamber.

Duval spoke to the others. "Go back to your posts," he commanded. Only Anton and the big man with the Luger remained behind.

The woman started to move away. "Koko—Rouge!"

"No—no, my dear, wait a moment!" And then to me, Duval inclined his head. "You are to go on a mission at once."

"*Oui*," I said. "But first, what of this Austin?"

He waved his hand, dismissing my question. "That will be taken care of."

"Good!" I said.

"Name the blackest country of Europe, monsieur."

I hesitated but a moment. "Spain," I said, thinking of their point of view. "All black. All Fascist," I said.

"Do you speak Spanish?"

"Well enough," I replied.

He spoke to the girl. "And you?"

"Perfectly—as you yourself should know."

"Of course," said Duval. "Then get the map."

Duval, Anton and the man with the Luger whom they had called Estuardo sat down at the table. I sat with them. The girl moved to the second room.

"We have had orders to send you at once to Madrid," Duval said. "Have you ever been in Spain before?"

"Several times."

"Then you know, the country and the people," Anton said.

"My answer would depend on what is asked of me."

"A great deal, monsieur, and of great importance."

I shrugged. "Is there ever a time when it is not important, always important?" I suggested with just enough weariness in my voice to allow them to jump on me. They jumped.

"That is not the right attitude," Duval said in a half scream, jumping up from his chair. "You are a fighter in the ranks, monsieur. Remember your oath. Remember it well!"

I made my face look properly chastened for this lapse from discipline. "I apologize, monsieur. But I am tired."

"We are all tired," Anton said.

"*Oui.* And do not forget!" snapped Duval.

I slumped into my chair. "I beg your forgiveness."

They did not reply. The girl came back then with several maps. Duval took them and spread the three large sheets on the table. He motioned me to come around.

He stared at the map and then up at me. Estuardo and Anton were on either side of me. Duval slapped the map with the back of his hand. "Madrid."

My eye quickly sought out familiar landmarks. I nodded.

He looked at me with a bemused expression. "Are you aware of the manner in which the leaders of the Revolution financed their revolutionary operations?"

He could not mean the Spanish Revolution, not with the emphasis he put on *the*. I nodded. "They robbed banks and post offices." I thought I had better comment on that. "And it was a good way."

Correct! He slapped the map again. "We must do the same." He placed his finger on a shaded area near to Prado in Madrid. "This is the Banco de Popular Suiza."

I nodded that I understood. It is always good to salt it away while the salting is good. And it is traditional to sock it away in Switzerland while the grabbing is good. Why not a branch bank? Saves a lot of plane fare. It was a wonder to me that some of the South American strong boys had not thought of it sooner.

"What do you want me to do?" I asked.

"You are to go to Madrid at once with Maria." He pulled out the second map. It was a detailed drawing of the bank. The third map showed the elevations of the building and the buildings on either side. He put his finger on the roof of the building next to the bank." This is a dress shop. Maria will get a job there."

I turned to the girl. "You are Maria?"

"*Oui.*"

"The two of you had better start talking to each other in Spanish."

We both nodded. We greeted each other elaborately in Spanish.

He smiled in approval.

"You have six weeks to go to Madrid, make your plans and complete your mission. You are to report back to me on January first."

"What is the mission?" I asked, studying the maps. "And what assistance will I have?"

"I will give you the names of trusted friends to our cause that you can contact in Madrid. The mission—" He inclined his head to one side and studied me— "ah! That is truly something, monsieur."

I waited. He turned to Anton. "Make copies of these at once. Have them ready to leave with then at dawn."

Anton nodded and left.

Then Duval asked, "What do you know of a man who calls himself Benedicto?"

The name meant something to me, but I wasn't sure what. I tugged at my lower lip. "I'm not sure."

"But you have heard the name?"

"Eustaquio Benedicto, monsieur?" I asked, not at all sure.

"The same. The cleverest smuggler and thief on the continent of Europe."

Eustaquio Benedicto. Almost a myth. But he was strictly a common criminal, probably wanted by all the police of Europe. I remembered hazy facts. Uncertain background, appeared on the French Riviera before the war, disappeared during it, and then showed up again after the war was over. He was then operating a fleet of small slow merchant ships out of southern France running to the near east and Africa, once in a while going to Spain. It was never clear, as I remembered it, just where he got the money to finance the purchase of the ships, not any of them more than three thousand tons.

I must have looked as if I knew something for Duval smiled. "You remember talk, eh?"

"Yes."

"Benedicto has retired from his smuggling of dope and transportation of white women to the Near East, to the Arabian countries, which as you know, still have slaves."

"I know." I said grimly. And it wasn't for his sake that I felt that way. I had contact with an Arab group while on a pursuit. I had watched one evening while my host had beaten an African to a bloody pulp for spilling hot food on his master.

"Benedicto had protection, of course. No one could have operated so openly, so flagrantly as he did without some sort of official status. We are not interested in this. There are vermin, monsieur, who will do anything for money with which they can satisfy their lusts." Duval finished out of breath. He had been almost screaming.

For a moment Duval's outrage sounded so genuine that I was tempted to believe him. But to me, Duval was not much better than Benedicto or my erstwhile Arab "master" host. They were after the same thing. They wanted to have people jump.

I waited for him to get his breath. "Monsieur. The mission."

"*Oui*. The mission." He nodded. He wiped his mouth with a handkerchief. "Benedicto has a huge fortune. He lives in Madrid nearby on a ranch." Duval sneered. "He is an aficionado of the bull ring. He raises bulls." He spit on the floor.

"The mission, monsieur," I said easily.

"The amount, monsieur, that this pig controls is thirty-eight million Swiss francs. It is in the form of bearer bonds. Thirty-eight of them, in a safety deposit box in the Banco de Popular Suiza." He straightened up. "You have until January first to get those bonds and deliver them to me in Paris."

"That is not much time, monsieur," I said, glancing at Maria. "A safety deposit box—" I shrugged. "Even if one had the key they must know Señor Benedicto."

"Silence!" Duval said. "You are not to question me in such a manner."

I said nothing.

"You refuse to go?" He asked softly, leaning on the table and looking at me. "Do you refuse?"

"I didn't say that, monsieur." I glanced at Maria. "You said I would have help."

"The names will be given to you," Duval said.

"Is that all the information you can give me?" I asked, trying hard to keep the honest incredulousness out of my voice. They didn't want much. There were a hundred and ten different ways to be caught, imprisoned, killed in an operation like this. In the Department, on a pursuit comparable to what Duval was asking me to do, there would be weeks and months of preparations. Here he gave me a girl and two dogs and the promise of some names of questionable value to help me in the outright robbery of thirty-eight million Swiss francs' worth of bonds—and from the vaults of a bank!

"When do we leave?" I said.

"When the maps are ready. Can you think of anything you might need before you go? Something—"

"I need nothing, monsieur!" I said sharply.

"Then I suggest you try and get some sleep. It will be dawn soon and you must leave here before dawn."

"Why?"

"No one comes or goes in the daylight, monsieur. Not even I."

"No one except he that drives the car, eh?" I said.

"You see too much. You observe too much. I still do not entirely trust you, Monsieur Nash. And when I return to Paris, I will make investigations."

"I'm sure you will, Monsieur Duval. But don't make the mistake of ever doubting me again. Or I might begin to doubt myself."

"Meaning what?"

"That I do not leave this cottage until I have written, specific orders as to the mission. That is to cover myself, monsieur. I am still on *another* mission, remember. I called you for help on that mission. The capture of Paul Austin. And you now countermand that order. You now give me another mission. I must have proof."

"Of what?"

"That I was ordered to go into Spain and behave like a common thief."

"You talk bravely now that you have been accepted," Duval said. I had been waiting for something along those lines. But I was ready.

"Naturally, monsieur. I have been approved. Not by you, but by the one that drives the car."

That shook him to his boots.

"It was his order that prevented me from being executed, and not yours. Wasn't it, Duval? Eh? So, not knowing who *he* is, I'm afraid I must have orders from you. *Official* orders."

I had not missed the return of Anton. Estuardo and Maria listened to me. Anton nodded his head. "I agree with him, Duval. If he was on another mission, he must have his orders."

Duval looked at Anton. He stood. "Have you copied the maps?"

"They are being prepared."

"Very well." He looked at his watch and turned to Maria. "Do you feel well enough to travel, mademoiselle?"

"*Oui.*" She looked at me.

"Estuardo will take you across the border to Spain. He will make arrangements to meet you once a week for a report that will be sent back to me. Estuardo will put you in contact with our people in Barcelona. And from there you will be escorted—and watched throughout the entire time you are there. Do not think, monsieur, that, once you have the bonds, you can escape us should you get such ideas. You are free—but you are not free, do you understand, Monsieur Nash?" He spit on the floor. "From the moment you leave here, someone will be watching you always!"

Anton and Estuardo shuffled their feet. Maria soothed the dogs with a word.

"Who will watch the watcher?" I asked harshly.

"Others will watch, and others watching them. It goes, monsieur, it goes and it goes. There is no end. Do not fail. Do not think there is a moment that you can escape one of us."

He walked out of the cottage without another word.

We sat very still, all of us, for a long while. Anton spoke first. His voice was heavy and muffled; his words, French with heavy Italian accents on the vowels, were sympathetic. "If you can think of things you might need, monsieur," he said helpfully.

"Ask Maria," I said. I patted my stomach where the butt of the .45 was showing. "I have all I need."

She shrugged. "I need nothing," she said quietly.

Estuardo stood. "Try and sleep," he said to both of us. "We will be leaving soon, and it is a long walk."

He and Anton left the room. I looked at Maria. She smiled. She raised a glass of wine. "Your health." She spoke in Spanish.

"And yours, señorita." I replied. "Good luck."

"Sí. To both of us."

But she did not look as if she believed there would be good luck. She returned to the room, the dogs behind her, and closed the door. I was alone.

It was a long way to go to clear a man's name. But if that is where you have to go, you go there. Right, Monty? I asked myself.

"It is so," I said aloud.

Chapter Nine

I SLEPT, but it was the bad kind. There were dreams of deep dark holes that kept pulling me down. Once I ended up in the arms of an aunt from Sandusky. She had a wart on her nose. I woke up fast.

It was still dark. I looked at my watch. Quarter to four. There would be time yet to leave. I lit a cigarette and cupped the flare of the match. I saw her then, sitting opposite me in the room. The dogs were not there.

"How is your shoulder?" I asked in Spanish.

"I had to get up," she replied in curling, lisping Castilian—but not heavy or studied.

"Are you Spanish?" I asked.

"I am from Segovia."

"You are a long way from home, señorita."

"Many of us are long way from home, Señor Nash."

"Please call me Monty," I said.

"Monty. It means Montgomery?"

"Yes."

"You were in a dangerous position, before *he* came in the car."

"It would seem so."

"You spoke well."

"I spoke the truth."

"That is not hard. Some say it is hard to speak the truth, but I have never found it hard."

"Can I get you anything?"

"No. Rest. It will be a long walk. And very difficult. We will be going soon. Koko—Rouge!" She called the dogs. They came out of the bedroom, stared at me and sat beside her.

"We have a difficult mission," I said, wondering what a young girl from Segovia was doing carrying the medallion. Helga had been right. There were more than the few that had been at Stalingrad. "Will *he* come again?"

"No."

"Who is he?" I asked boldly. It would be a natural question to ask under any circumstances.

"I do not know. Only Duval takes his orders," she said.

"How long have you carried the medallion?"

"Two years. It was given to me by my father before he died."

"Oh." I expressed my sympathy. "He would have been a *soldado*," I said. "There." I pressed a little on the there.

"*Sí*. That is where he got the medallion. They sent him to Spain when he was going to die. He gave me the medallion and told me of Duval and Anton."

"Anton is a good man," I said, knowing that she liked him.

"Do you think so, señor?" She asked, a little more vibrance to her voice.

"A good man. You should know that none but the best carry the *disco*."

"He brought my father to Segovia." She leaned forward. Her voice became stronger. "He has been like a father to me since then."

"You make me feel unworthy after the incident of your wound, señorita."

"You must not think of it. And you must call me Maria," she said.

Anton and Estuardo came in a few moments later. Both carried clothes and Estuardo had changed into a black business suit and wore a rain coat cape-style over his shoulders. Maria went into the bedroom and closed the door. I began to strip and put on the obviously Spanish style clothes.

"Estuardo will take you across the border—" Anton began.

"Yeah, I know," I said. "But that's all he does."

"Meaning what, señor?" Estuardo demanded.

"Meaning that the responsibility for the completion of the mission Duval assigned me is in my hands. Not anyone else's. If I do not like the way you lead me across the border, then I will go my own way. With the woman."

They didn't like that. But I didn't care whether they liked it or not. I wasn't going to stick my head in so far that I couldn't get it out. And I wanted Maria to understand how I felt. I had not forgotten the dogs. Dogs, in themselves are not difficult to avoid or kill. But when they are directed by a master they have been trained to obey and protect, that is another matter. If she sent them on me I would have to kill them. This I did not want to do. I already had a vague plan forming in the back of my head for the accomplishment of Duval's fantastic plan to hold up a bank in the heart of Madrid and steal—*steal* thirty-eight million in Swiss francs. The plan included the dogs.

"Señor," I said, facing Estuardo, "you are no doubt a good man. You will probably get me across the border safely. But I wanted you to know that you are not the leader. Is it understood?"

"He is right," Maria said from the door. She now wore a chic dress and a topcoat. Her arm was no longer in a sling, but she rested it by keeping her hand in the pocket of the coat. She was even more beautiful and enchanting than before. The dogs were at her side.

Her words were unexpected, but very welcome. They knew her and obviously had faith in her. I smiled. "Señorita!" I said and inclined my head.

Anton and Estuardo withdrew to one side while I completed my dressing. Maria returned to the bedroom.

Nothing more was said until we were outside the cottage. Then Anton spoke.

"Estuardo will take you across the border and put you in touch with people. They will help you."

"I need the password," I said.

"Estuardo will give it to you once you are across the border."

"A lot of things can happen to Estuardo before we *reach* the border. A rock could fall from a peak and land on his hard head."

"When you are across the border, Señor Nash," Estuardo said.

"Now!" I said.

"You are being dangerously stubborn," said Anton.

"Stubborn, but not too dangerously. You know I'm right. What happens if Estuardo and I are separated? Does the mission fail because you were too cautious to give me the password?" I laughed. "Señor Anton, what is there for me to gain by knowing the expression now?"

"*Zurrapa.*" Maria said joining my side. "The dregs, señor."

They looked at her angrily. But I knew she had told me the truth. I nodded. "Señorita," I said, "*Zurrapa.*"

"Come!" Estuardo said gruffly. "We must hurry."

***

We walked for an hour and a half through pitch-black night and unbroken trails. There were no lights or landmarks that I could see, but I had the odd sensation that we were traveling in a circle. The dogs took turns roving ahead and behind, while one stayed with Maria. She held us back, stopping several times to rest.

About the time it grew gray in the east, we were on an open trail. And by full dawn we were on a small road that was leading us past several thatched farmhouses. I saw no one, but memorized the countryside. At seven in the morning we were in a village.

"Cortile," Estuardo said. "We will take a car here and drive to Cuneo."

"Then what?" I asked.

"The train to Nice."

"I do not have papers," I said at once.

"That will be taken care of," he said abruptly."

We walked through the heart of the village that was no more than half a dozen thatched houses on either side of the lane. I saw no one, but I knew we were being watched. Several times I saw the curtains at the windows fall as I turned my head unexpectedly.

At the end of the line Estuardo stopped and motioned us to wait. He went around to the back of the barn, and in a few minutes I heard the stuttering cough of an engine kicking over. And in another minute he pulled around the side of the barn in a badly dented and beaten-up French Renault. Maria got into the back with the dogs and I sat behind Estuardo.

The road leveled out onto a plain and soon in the distance I could see the old fortress city of Cuneo. It has been a busy city for centuries, and it was no less busy as we drove through the tortured, narrow streets. I saw no reason for stopping the car where he did, but Estuardo braked and cut the engine.

We were near the *bazar* and the farmers were bringing their vegetables and foodstuffs to be sold. On either side of us were the immense walls of a decaying fortress that might have once withstood siege when Cuneo owed allegiance to the House of Savoy.

We sat for an hour. Nothing happened. It began to grow cold in the car, and the dogs became restless. I was about to suggest that Maria and I get out and stretch our legs when a man in a shapeless rag of a coat and old, moth-eaten beret came to the side of the car. He lingered a moment and then tossed something onto Estuardo's lap. He opened it, read it and grunted.

"This way," he said, getting out. We stepped out into the stream of human traffic, were jostled and stared at and avoided because of the dogs that were now on leash and held tightly by Maria's one good arm.

We followed Estuardo down the street, turned into a small alley and walked up a flight of stairs. We were let into a small dingy office, and Maria sank into the nearest chair.

An old man came out of the back, spoke to Estuardo and looked at us. "Everything is arranged. We only need the pictures."

"Come," Estuardo said gruffly . We were led into the back room where all three of us sat for our photographs. When this was done the old man showed us into still another room and called for a boy to bring food.

Maria would not eat until the dogs had been fed. She refused bread for them and demanded meat. The old man was reluctant, but he finally had the boy bring out a half joint of mutton. Maria cut it into equal parts and fed it to Koko and Rouge. Then she sat down to eat with Estuardo and myself.

A steady diet of bread, cheese and wine may be good for the European, but my tastes also ran to something a little more bloody. I swilled the wine, washing down the dry bread and cheese, and looked on hungrily while the damn dogs gorged themselves on the mutton.

A half hour later the old man came out with Italian passports. They were excellent. The seal was perfect. I wondered how he was able to do it and made a note of the address and his name, which Estuardo had tried hard to prevent me from hearing when he spoke with him.

Maria and I compared pictures and laughed at the inexorable stiffness found in all passport photos. The old man came out a second time, carrying with him health certificates for the dogs. These too were so cleanly done that they looked like the genuine paper. Estuardo and the old man began discussing money.

Estuardo paid him off. He was more than pleased. I could understand why. He was paid in Swiss francs, some of those I had taken from de Loon and that Anton and the others had taken from me. It was the first time that I had thought about money. I then remembered the huge diamond ring that I had taken from Helga's jewelry box. I slipped my finger into my watch pocket—and then cursed. I had left it in the trousers I had taken off at the cottage.

I was still looking at Estuardo and the old man, and suddenly I saw the ring. Estuardo was wearing it on his little finger. I did not say anything until we were back on the street and walking toward the railroad station. I stepped ahead of Maria and to Estuardo's side.

"Give me the ring." I said.

"What?" He said.

"The ring. You took it from me. It is on your finger."

He glanced at me guiltily. "It is not your ring."

"I can take it from you, señor," I said as harshly as I could. "But I would prefer that you just return it to me." And then I added with a tone of disgust. "I despise *thieves!*"

He looked at me. "There is no need to get nasty."

"Give me the ring."

"You are making a mistake," he said.

"No, señor. You are making the mistake. I can understand if the *grupo* took the money. The society always needs money. That is the nature of the mission, señor. But you have taken *personal* property. Give me the ring."

He stopped. Maria began to suspect that something was wrong. We stood on the edge of the square facing the railroad station.

"What is it?" She asked.

I looked straight at Estuardo. "He is a thief. He has taken a ring from me."

Maria turned and looked at Estuardo in disbelief. He was too flustered to hide it. "I remember there was something about a ring—" She said.

I didn't mind going to Spain and trying to work a fantastic robbery if it would lead me to the leader, or if it would get me to the point where I might know more about the organization of medallion carriers. I knew that somewhere in this society there was an answer to Paul's supposed defection. I knew, too, that GloSec Europe had no idea that the medallion society even existed. And it was, as far as I could learn, a vast, sprawling network of dedicated men and women who would do anything commanded. For some reason that I did not know, for some pure chance perhaps, I had been selected to assume the Madrid operation. If I was successful, possession of thirty-eight million in Swiss bearer bonds would be an ace card to hold in digging into the organizational records. Somewhere in those records was proof of Paul's innocence—and of my own. With thirty-eight million Swiss francs in bonds, they would come to me. But I did not want to be watched every minute by Estuardo—or by any of his companions in Spain. Estuardo had proven the one thing that I was most afraid of. I could not trust him. What would happen to Montgomery Nash when he had those bonds in his hands? Would he then be taken by the hand and lead back to Paris where he would deliver the same bonds into Duval's greedy little hands? Like hell he would.

I had had ideas of dumping Estuardo when we had crossed the border into Spain. I had been thinking about some reason that would satisfy Maria and at the same time put Estuardo on the defensive. I had not expected it to happen so soon.

"Estuardo!" She said. There was shock and pain in her voice.

"Señorita!"

"Give me the ring, thief!" I said again.

He bristled. I let him get tough. He dropped his hand on the Luger.

"You wouldn't pull that gun, señor." I said. "Maria would have the dogs on you in an instant." He hesitated. I held out my hand. "I do not choose to carry on with you, señor. Maria," I said, without taking my eyes away from his, "I am going on alone. I know ways to cross the border. The French-Italian border as well as the Spanish border. If you wish to come with me, very well. But I will not go on with a thief who steals from his comrades!"

"Señor—Monty!" She said.

I turned. There was a small crowd around us. I had been too worked up to think of the scene I was causing, there on the street. Anyone could see that there was some kind of trouble. I saw the policeman walking toward us.

"Go to the station at once, Maria." I said quickly. "And you, thief, give me the ring and the money quick!"

He glanced fearfully toward the approaching policeman. He slipped the ring from his finger and reached inside his pocket. His hand hesitated on the Luger. I dropped my hand on the butt of the .45. "Try it, señor," I said through my teeth. He shifted his hand and brought out the money and the passports. I shoved them into my pocket. The crowd was pressing in on top of us now, but no one was close enough to see what had happened. I saw that Maria was just entering the station.

"Now run!" I said to Estuardo. "It is the only way to prevent an investigation!"

He glanced around. There was fear in his eyes. "Run?" He asked stupidly.

"Run! There must be no questions asked of me or Maria! *Run!*"

The policeman was only fifty feet away now. "You must create a diversion, quick! Run!"

Fear of me, or perhaps fear that he may have lead us into a situation that would negate the mission and he would have to answer to—who? All of this, and the fear of the policeman was in his eyes and a moment before he turned to run, he pleaded with me.

I clenched my teeth. "Run, thief!" I said.

He turned and ran. I stepped back. The crowd murmured. He was racing through the square, back toward the bazar. I looked at the policeman. I pointed. "Thief! Thief!"

The crowd surged after Estuardo. Suddenly the scene in the square, a moment before peaceful and orderly, dissolved into a wild race after Estuardo. And in the lead the policeman.

I saw Maria in the window of the station. I pointed to the far end of the square. She nodded. I began walking toward the street corner, my eye on a car. Maria came out of the station. I walked a little faster. We met near the car. "How soon will the train be here?" I asked hurriedly.

"Not for an hour."

"Get in." I opened the door of the car, looking around for the owner. She ordered the dogs inside and I slipped under the wheel. The motor kicked over and I shot the car into gear. We roared off down the street. I drove two blocks with one eye on the rearview mirror. No one shouted at us, and no one followed us.

I turned a corner and stopped before a garage. I got out and walked over to the attendant. "Can you have the car washed and filled with gas and oil in two hours?" I asked.

The man nodded that he could. I handed him the keys and watched him while he pulled the car into the garage. Maria and I walked away.

"They will be looking for the car," I said. "Cuneo is not so large that it would not be found within a few minutes. And there is only one main road to the south towards France."

"What of Estuardo?" She asked. "What if they catch him."

"They will let him go when there is no one to accuse him," I said.

I could see the relief on her face. "We must get out of town at once," I said. "And we need a car."

"We can take the train. It stops at a small station several kilometers out of town," she said. "We could walk there."

We had been speaking Spanish. I now told her to speak French. It would not be as obvious this close to the border, and I explained, "The dogs. They are a giveaway. We must travel by car."

She nodded. "But it would not be wise to steal an automobile."

"I will get one," I said. "Wait in that café."

She nodded.

"Hold on. Do you have a gun?"

She patted Rouge's head. "For what, Monty?" She smiled.

I went back to the garage. I explained to the attendant that I would need my car at once, unless he had a car he could rent me while my own was being cared for. He had one. A big Alfa that he rolled out and that he said was his own, promising me that it was in top condition. It proved later to be just as he had said. I paid him several hundred Swiss francs, which he was happy to accept, and drove back to the café. Maria got into the car.

"To Spain," I said, and grinned at her.

She did not smile back. She spoke to Koko and Rouge and made them sit in the back. Then she placed her head against her arm, leaned against the door and went to sleep.

I drove the big Alfa hard and in a few minutes we were in the Maritime Alps. It is beautiful county. The roads there are good and the Alfa was a powerful old car. I hated to leave it, but I was not going to trust the passports. Estuardo may have thought over what I had done to him and told the police. That wasn't likely, but I could not afford to take the chance.

I also hated to awaken Maria. But she did not seem to mind when I told her we would have to make it across the border on foot.

***

We waited until dark, sleeping most of the day hidden in a dense thicket of brush that overlooked the border station. It lay on a hill to our left and I watched the cars move back and forth through the candy-striped barriers until the light faded and the traffic was evident only by the beam of headlights and the grinding of gears as the cars moved out again.

I had a plan in mind, intending to work out of the thicket as soon as it was dark and go directly to the station itself.

I wore the .45 in my side pocket now. I did not want to shoot, but I was not going to be taken. I woke Maria. Her arm was sore and she felt hot. I thought she might have a fever and insisted on looking at the wound. I uncovered it and saw that Anton was right.

It was only a flesh wound that had cut about a three-quarter-inch wedge into the shoulder muscle. It was a nasty wound but a day or two of rest would put it right. It was clean, so there was no worry.

I dressed it as well as I could, careful, not to bind it too tightly. She watched me, looking into my face, apparently not at all bothered by being half-undressed before me. She was so small and so delicately put together. I found myself wondering how and why a girl like Maria would be so deep in a thing as complex and unstable as the medallion society. But this was no time to question her. And it was no time to think about anything but getting across the border.

Her only comment when I had finished and helped her slip the top of her dress back over her shoulder was quiet and direct. "You are very gentle, señor," she said. And it made me feel good.

"We may have to run a short distance. Are you well enough for that?" I asked.

She nodded.

I pointed toward the border station. The traffic continued to roll back and forth. Riviera traffic—sports cars and fun-loving passengers moving from San Remo to Monte Carlo. "There are two barriers," I said. "Italian and French. Two men in each pillbox."

She nodded. I pointed to a dark spot several hundred yards to the right of the barrier and along the border. "There is where we will cross. When they are busy with cars on both sides, I want you to send Koko and Rouge through the gates. That will draw attention to them. We will then cross."

I helped her up, and we walked across the open field to a small depression and stopped. I waited until there were several cars on either side of the station. The border was two hundred yards away. "Now," I said.

She spoke to the dogs and pointed. They responded instantly. They started off toward the station at top speed.

We headed for the dark spot and the border. The dogs bounded around the waiting cars and went on through. The motorists began to shout. The guards stopped their checking of the papers and turned their attention to the dogs. There was a moment of confusion—which was all I needed—and we were across and into France.

A second later the area for a thousand yards up and down the border and around it was lighted brilliantly. But we were safely across.

"How will you locate Koko and Rouge?" I asked.

"They will locate me," she said.

And they did. We were on the outskirts of Menton, walking along the highway, when we heard the padding feet and the panting of the dogs. They stepped lightly to her side and received a pat on the head from her. Then they trotted alongside us.

In Menton I stole a Volkswagen because there were so many of them. I changed the plates, shifting them from one car to another four times and drove back to the outskirts of town where I picked up Maria.

**

It is roughly three hundred miles from Menton, France on the Italian border to Puigcerda, Spain just over the border from France. It was a full day before we began the climb into the Pyrenees, and noon when I hid the car in a small mountain cave. Maria was exhausted from the hard driving, and I was in need of sleep. Crossing the border had been simple once before in a pursuit into Spain. I hoped it was going to prove as simple with an exhausted woman. I had stopped in Marseilles during the trip, buying food and wine. Koko and Rouge had ranged the area, stretching their legs after the long ride in the car. Maria had disappeared too. I prepared the simple lunch and waited. She did not appear. Koko was back and asleep, but Rouge had disappeared. I stood. Koko was alert at once. I walked off into the thick stand of trees and called, "Maria!" I listened. There was no reply. I walked on. Koko remained at my side for another hundred yards and then bounded ahead of me. In a moment I heard the sound of running water. I stopped, located it to my right and moved through the thin undergrowth, through the trees.

Maria was nude, standing knee-deep in a quiet pool of clear mountain water. She was talking softly to Rouge, inviting him into the water, her voice light and gay. She turned and the sun caught the wetness of her thighs. She was facing me, but she did not see me because of the trees and the sun. She drank from the pool, then splashed water at the dog. The dog barked and lunged on the edge of the pool. And then I heard her laugh. She stood erect, twisting her slim body, and ran splashing after the dog. She disappeared. I turned away, stumbling, my breath coming hard, feeling the sweat leap to the palms of my hands. I returned to the camp site and sat down. It took a long time for me to forget that slim, young, beautiful body in a mountain pool. She returned, her hair dripping, and sat down without a word to begin eating hungrily. "We start early in the morning," I said to her. "Once before I crossed here. One must endeavor to reach the heights and the passes about noon when the sun is the hottest. I crossed once at night and a compatriot had his toes frozen. It is too late in the day to start now."

She slept most of the day while I searched for firewood, but there was little to be had. The ranges had been picked clean by many others, very many others, in the centuries before me. I found a cave before dark and went back to wake her. "We must keep a fire going all night," I explained. "We are still high enough to freeze."

The dark came down on us swiftly, terribly. The dogs, lying in the cave's entrance, seemed my friends now.

She sat before the fire and sipped some wine. The cave grew warm and she relaxed. She turned to me, stood and slowly undressed in the firelight, watching my eyes on her body. "I saw you watching me in the pool," she said softly. "I'm glad you waited —"

She was in my arms, her mouth on mine, searching, tasting of wine, her lithe young body flecked by the dark red firelight. She murmured something in Spanish and then gripped me fiercely. I found myself forgetting about Paul, medallions, spies... She drew me down onto the coat she had spread on the floor of the cave. The wind began to blow outside, but there, where I was, there was no wind, no sound except the sounds that lovers make — ages old but ever new.

***

She lay in my arms and we looked at the fire, sipping wine, being quiet and thoughtful. We were both thinking of the thing that had brought us together in this cave at this time. She had sighed. She had wondered loud about pain, asked about it the way a child will ask about where there is the moon. Only she asked why there had to be pain at all.

"There is a reason for all this, señorita," I said gently. I kissed her cheek. She held my hand cupped under one delicate, small, perfectly formed breast. "At a moment like this, it is very hard to understand why such pain, such effort must be endured. But there is a reason. Many have died for it."

I was talking truth, only I did not speak of it. I thought about the Fox squads that had gone on a pursuit and had never returned. I thought about the terrible suffering endured by those same Fox Squads. There was a lesson somewhere in what I was doing with my life. Some great truth that if discovered would certainly help those who make The Decisions.

"I *know* why I carry the medallion, Señor. I know the reasons. But they are not reasons that come out of books. They are not *idea* reasons. They are—"

She stopped. There was a noise near us. The dogs' ears stood, and Rouge got up. Koko straightened in her long stretch, pulling her hind legs up behind her. Rouge lunged off to investigate. In a moment he returned with a rabbit in his mouth.

Maria patted the big dog and took the rabbit away from him. She put it to one side and would not let either of them have it. "Tomorrow," she promised them. "They will sleep if they have eaten," she said.

"What reasons, Maria?" I asked.

"I will show you—in time, señor. It is something you must see." She spoke to the dogs. "Stand guard! Koko! Rouge!"

"You will show it to me?"

"I promise," she said. "Koko! Rouge!" The dogs stood, alert.

I slept little that night, but enough to keep from falling on my face the next morning. At dawn we began the climb and by three in the afternoon we were in Puigcerda. We caught a local train to Barcelona and at ten that night crawled aboard an express that would take us through Caspe, Zaragoza, Siguenza and into the great plain that is the center of Spain and its heart, Madrid.

There were no incidents. We traveled as Señor and Señora Bernardo. In Madrid we checked into a small hotel in the eastern section of the city that was not damaged during the civil war and that still has the charm of being old and cheap.

We went out that night and found a doctor for Maria's shoulder. The wound had been cleaned well by Anton back in the Italian mountains. The doctor said there was nothing more to be done. We bought bandages at a drugstore and headed back to the hotel.

I left her a block from the Hotel Granada. "Go to your room. I will contact you."

"But—" There was a look of disappointment in her eyes. And then she quickly covered it. She compressed her lips and nodded her head. "*Sí.*"

"I'll see you tomorrow," I said gently. "*Adios.*"

"*Adios,*" she said and touched my cheek.

I turned from her beautiful face and into the night of Madrid. A city of medieval attitudes to play against a city of contradictions that stretched across a thousand years of cruel history. The cry for blood rings out in no city like that of Madrid. When one walks through the Madrid night one hears that cry.

I was aware that she had wanted me to, had expected me to take her again, that night, in the quiet and luxury of a bed. But I would have her again.

I bumped into a stranger as I dashed for a cab. "Pardon."

"Sure, Monty," the voice said.

Chapter Ten

ORRICK AND SHELDON were on either side of me before I could move. They hustled me into the cab. There was no use in trying to get away from them. Orrick was the best judo man I've ever known.

"Pretty stupid of you to turn up in a capitol, wasn't it, Monty?" Sheldon said. I had always disliked him. And the feeling had been mutual. He was one of those agents in the Agency who felt the weight of the world on their shoulders twenty-four hours a day. And they cried about it. Sheldon was, however, a good agent. Orrick had been Fox Leader of their first squad for four years. "Be quiet, Shelly," he said.

"You just bumped into me," I said. "You couldn't have known I would show up here." I cursed my luck under my breath.

"Able Head has every first squad in GloSec out looking for you." Orrick replied. He leaned across me and gave an address to the driver. He settled back. "Rex wants you."

"And he's going to get you," Sheldon said.

"Shut up, Shelly," Orrick said. "How about it, Monty. Want to tell us how you got here and what you've been doing since you belted Rex and ducked out of Worthington Gardens?"

I said nothing.

"Yeah, double-crosser, let's have the story," Shelly said. He ran his hands over me and came up with the .45. He smelled it. "Who'd you shoot?"

"A sparrow," I said.

"Wise guy. I never liked you, Nash. I like you even less now that you're a lousy creep."

"Have you learned anything about Paul?" I asked Orrick.

"Sure we have," Sheldon replied. "He's a creep like you."

"You know I can't say anything, Monty," Orrick said. I got the feeling that he did not like the idea of having to pick me up. That was the wrong attitude. It gave me the edge. He should be like Sheldon, I thought, ready to kick my teeth out at the slightest chance. "Got anything else on you?" He asked.

"Phony passport and about three thousand in cash," I said.

"Let's have it," Sheldon said. He ran his hands through my pocket and came out with the papers and money. He looked at them in the light of his cigarette lighter. "Pretty good. Who did them?"

"The same sparrow," I said. I turned sideways. "Don't talk to me, crumb. Let a good agent question me."

"Crumb!" Sheldon laughed. He didn't get mad. He was wise. He didn't take a poke at me in the back seat of the car with three guys riding. If he had there was the chance that I might reach his shoulder holster.

Orrick had the papers. He studied them and counted the money. "Anything else, Monty?"

"No," I lied. The medallion was in my shoe.

"I'm taking your word, Monty."

"I said there wasn't anything else, Orrick," I said, getting as much honesty in my voice as I could."

I had to get away from them. I had to move before they got me to wherever they were taking me. It would be a mock-up joint for Spain headquarters. But it might as well be the federal pen in Atlanta. I knew such places. I would never get out.

I couldn't handle both of them. Someway I had to get them separated. And in spite of Orrick's judo ability, I preferred him to Sheldon. Orrick was slightly hesitant, with a disgust for me and my alleged defection. If it came to a fight, it wouldn't take him long to get over it. Instinct would take over after the first blow. But I wouldn't need more than one blow. Just one, if it was clean and unencumbered. I could take him.

"I'm supposed to meet a guy in two hours," I said, trying to get weariness into my voice.

"Where?"

"It's not so much where, but what he'll be carrying," I said.

"Like what? Explosives to blow up the Prado?" Sheldon laughed. "Don't hand me that—"

"Sheldon the big mouth hit it. There was a meet set up to work over one of the power plants in southern Madrid—"

Sheldon laughed harshly. "Fade that one, Orrick. From big time super-spy to blowing up power plants!"

Orrick wasn't giving Sheldon much fun. He cracked down hard. "Leave your personal feelings out of this, Shelly. And cut out those cracks." Once again he turned to me and there was a sigh before he spoke. "Well?" He was weak, I registered thoughtfully. And if I ever got out of this, I would tell Rex so. He should be hard with me, I thought, like Rex was hard and Guardian was hard, not ready to believe anything. Sheldon was playing it smart.

"It was a job. One they knew I could do well. I've scouted the plant. It's the main booster for most of Madrid—take that one out and most of the juice in town goes with it. And for a good three or four days."

"What good would that do?" Sheldon demanded.

"Riots, strikes, general disorder," I said.

"But what *good* would that do?" Orrick asked.

"You never can tell. A lot of people start milling around in the streets and the soldiers are brought out to keep them moving. Someone gets knocked down, maybe cut up with a kite knife by a soldier, or maybe shot. That makes the mobs see red. They attack. They have to bring out the tanks, then the planes and before you know it the whole government is spending most of its time putting down strikes and riots in the streets."

"And it all adds up to nothing," Sheldon said.

"Two hours, you said," Orrick snapped. There was a little more metal to his voice now. "What's the man's name?"

"I don't know. We have a greeting."

"What's the greeting?" Sheldon demanded.

"Big Noise," I replied.

"That all?" Orrick asked.

"He'll wear a big overcoat. He'll have the stuff on him."

"What stuff?"

"Nitro."

"Jesus Christ! He's going to carry it *on* him? In his *pocket*?" Sheldon asked.

"Where else? In his hat, you stupid bastard?"

I let him slap me without ducking away. Orrick reached over pulled him back. "That's enough, Shelly!" He turned to the driver of the car. "Slow down and stop at the next corner."

"Where's the meet?" Orrick asked me.

"The south entrance—" I stopped. I didn't want to give it to them too fast. As it was I was afraid they would get wise to my splitting them up. And I didn't want them to go for help, though there was nothing in the world to stop them from just making a phone call to the city police and letting them handle it.

Sheldon slapped me again. "Let's have it, creep," he said.

"The south entrance to what, Monty?" Orrick demanded.

"Buen Retiro Park," I said finally.

The cab stopped. Sheldon had the door open. "I'll handle it, and I hope the bastard falls and trips and blows himself to hell if he had anything to do with you."

"Wait a minute, Shelly!" Orrick said as Sheldon was about to slam the door. "No need in our getting mixed up in it. Call Sergeant Ortiga. Let the local dicks take him."

"Yeah. Maybe you're right. I'll call." He strode rapidly toward a nearby cafè.

It would take about three minutes for him to make the call and return.

Three minutes. I had to get Orrick off guard. I started to talk. I went back and made up a fantastic beginning about Paul and I defecting. He listened. I kept my eyes on the door of the cafè. It seemed to me that the three minutes had long since passed—and then I started to cry.

It was the first time in my life that I had been able to shed tears on demand. Orrick was not looking at me. He had slumped down in his seat and was staring out the window on his side. I had leaned over on the seat, blubbering, when suddenly I sprang at him.

I went for his throat, got it and pressed hard. I counted. One-two-three-four-five-six-seven-eight-nine-ten—and then I let go. He was under. Choking and fighting to come out from under it. And then he let me have his right elbow, arm doubled, stiff and straight. He winged me under the chin, and I went back. But I was stronger than he was and shook it off. I went back and chopped him once on the Adam's apple, and he was through.

I took his gun and the money he had taken from me. I searched for the two spare clips to the .45 all of us carried. I got them out of his pocket just as Sheldon was coming out of the cafè. I pulled Orrick upright and held him up on the seat, watching the approaching Sheldon. The driver had not even turned around. I doubt he heard us through his glass partition.

I held the .45 ready as Sheldon opened the door. "All set. Ortiga will take care of—" He stopped. He tried to slam the door, but I had my foot up ready for that one.

"Get in the car," I said between my teeth. I shoved the .45 in his face as he bent over. I pulled out his gun and the one he had taken from me. I shoved them into my pocket. "Tell him to take us back to the Prado and then lie down on the floor."

"Back to the Prado," he said to the driver. He lay down on the floor. I put my foot on his neck and pressed. Not hard, but just enough to make up for the two slaps, even though from his point of view I deserved them.

"The locals have got your boy sewed up tight in the park, creep," he said from the floor of the car.

"Get wise, Shelly. There wasn't any boy," I said. "Now you listen to me. You take a message back to Rex. You tell him to lay off me. You tell him that, or the next time any of you boys come up against me it won't be with a foot in the face but a good old American Army forty-five slug."

The car slowed for a light. I swung from the door and was out of the car and down the nearest dark lane in fifteen seconds.

They didn't try to follow me. It would have been suicide for them and they knew it.

I felt sorry for Orrick. He wouldn't be able to swallow for a week without cursing me and all my nearest and dearest relations.

Feeling like the arsenal at Philadelphia with three loaded .45's and four spare clips, I clanked my armed way down the lane to the nearest boulevard. I flagged another taxi and rode the twenty-odd miles to the town of Vallecas where I knew a man with a thick neck like a bull and whose name was Toro.

Chapter Eleven

HIS REAL NAME was Manuel Marte and he was, as far as I was concerned, the only man in Spain I could trust. I had met him during one of my pursuits in Spain several years before in, of all places, an art gallery. Manuel Marte was an artist. At the first meeting we had retired to a cafè and discussed art for nine solid hours.

He lived in a garden cottage on the estate of his patron, whom he cursed for lack of taste, for the immorality of being wealthy, for the lack of human values and for everything that Toro could think of except the money that was handed out to him regularly. The patron asked nothing in return except that Toro spend his life painting. This was agreeable since Toro would have done this anyway.

He knew nothing of my work and believed me to be a fellow artist. He greeted me with a bear hug that was unavoidable.

"What brings you to Spain, sènor? Are you in debt? If you are, my friend, go away. I will be your friend no longer. Money is the spawner of the *acadèmico*. Can you think for a moment, señor, what art the world would now have if there had been no money to influence the artist? *Puof!* I tell you, señor, if you are in need of money, go away."

"I don't want money. I have plenty of it." I showed him the thick package of Swiss francs. His eyes became wary.

Then you come for what? No one comes to visit Toro unless they want something. Of course you want something! You must tell me what it is and then I will decide if I will help you."

"I am going to rob a bank," I said simply.

"*Maravilloso!*" He bellowed, "I will help you all I can. Is it here in Spain? Is it to be done soon? How much will you get from the—" he scratched his head and thought of the word in English that would fit— "caper?"

I hesitated, but if he was going to help me, he would have to understand. And then for the first time in my years of training and life as an agent, I confessed. I told him everything. He listened to me with his eyes turning this way and that. He shook his head. He pounded the table. He pulled his hair and moaned as if he had been struck. He held his back and paced the floor. I told him only that I was a professional agent and that I had been accused of defecting. He listened to the murder of Helga, de Loon and the maid nervously. My outwitting of the medallion carriers in the Italian mountains sent him to biting his fingernails. He roared at the way I had ducked away from Estuardo. And when I told him of what had happened that night in Madrid he was laughing so hard his eyes were full of tears.

"That brings me to you, señor," I said at last. "You see now that I must do this fantastic thing—robbing the bank for the Swiss bonds—not for profit, but as bait to catch the bigger ones in the organization. As I told you, even my own people suspect me. But there is nothing I can do about that but behave as I did tonight and trust to luck. I cannot share the loot with you. It must be returned to the bank in time. But I must accomplish this mission for the medallion carriers and use it as bait."

He understood. And then he spoke. He wiped his eyes. "Señor, I am not political. I am sorry. I would be worthless to you on such a day. I am—" he shrugged his shoulders— "a big man. I have great strength, sí, but for things like this, I am a child."

"I ask very little," I said.

"It makes no difference. I am an artist. I can only do one thing—and there are those critics who say that I cannot even do that. I can paint! I can draw!" He drank a glass of wine without stopping. "I do not care if they shoot up the world tomorrow. I do not care. I have only two things that mean anything to me. They are there." He pointed to the room. "One is a woman. For the moment her name is Carlotta. Tomorrow or next week it might be something else. But for the moment, this moment, señor, I am in love with her. And the other thing beside her. It is the new painting, the one that I am working on now. And like the woman, it will be gone tomorrow or next week, but right now it is my universe, señor."

I nodded that I understood. I stood up. He did not look at me. "How will you get back to Madrid tonight? It is late. You had better stay here. Strange things happen in the streets at night. And especially for you." He shook his head. "You had better stay."

"No. I must find someone that will help me."

"I can't help you, señor!" He roared. "I am an artist, not a bank robber! *Madre Dios*!"

"I do not want you to rob a bank. All I want of you is to draw it for me," I said.

He stopped. "Draw the bank?"

"Inside. Every detail. And the distances."

He stared at me. "Draw the inside of the bank? Draw pictures of the bank for you?"

I pulled out the money. I held out a thousand francs for what I thought my expenses would come to and put the rest of it on the table. "This is your money. Take it to the Banco de Popular Suiza. Deposit it. Rent a safety deposit box and put anything you like into it. Valuable paintings. Money. Anything at all. Then go to the bank and take some of the money out. Put some of it in. Go in two, three—four times a week and make drawings of what you see. Make notes on how one is allowed to enter the safety deposit box vault—"

Toro held up his hand and nodded his head. "This I can do," he said. And then he began to apologize. "I had visions, señor of going up to the bank with a machine gun—" He looked at the money. "It is a strange world. It never fails to find a fascinated child in Toro the bull, señor. What you ask is little enough."

"No one knows I have been here. No one will know that I have been here. I will contact you during the Christmas week. Will that give you time enough?"

He nodded. His face suddenly grew serious. It was not the bluster that he used for his tirades against anything that he found annoying. This was a face that meant what it was about to say. "I do not know why I say I will help you."

"I think I know," I said.

"You cannot know. Perhaps I am political. If knowing the inner heart, señor, the true thing that is freedom—and who knows it better than the artist, who sees always far far ahead of the others—if this is political, then, señor, I am convicted of living a lie."

"That is only partly true, *amigo*."

"You are a terrible artist. But enough to understand. But you do not know."

"I know another way, Toro," I said.

"What do you know of freedom?"

"I was brought up, as the Romans said, freeborn."

"*Sí.*" He nodded. "You know. I will have the drawings ready for you."

"Christmas week."

"*Sí.* The week of Padre Noël."

He walked me to the road and into the edge of the city of Vallecas. The stars hung heavily over our heads in the bright, harsh night. He stared at them. "Is it done again, up there, on the stars, señor, as it is here? Is it done again and again and again, with people thinking their big and little thoughts?"

"I would like to think so," I said.

"Do they crawl or do they walk upright?" He asked, deep in his wonder.

"If they know freedom, whether they crawl or swing or fly or swim, they know the joy of living."

"That is all that's important," he agreed.

"All."

"Nothing more," he said with finality.

"Not unless you believe in God."

"Only the fool, señor, laughs in the face of this." He spread his arms wide and took in the universe. "Only the fool would dare laugh."

"Good night, Toro." I said as a taxi pulled up beside me.

"Good night. Padre Noël, *sí.*"

"Padre Noël, *sí.*"

I left him standing in his undershirt, studying the heavens as if he were seeing them for the first time. Toro, Bull, Manuel Marte. Bank Robber.

I slept all the way back to Madrid. And once there, I ate a good meal and began searching for names in the telephone book. I found the name of Eustaquio Benedicto.

All the way back to the Hotel Granada I thought about Eustaquio Benedicto and the key in his possession that would open the safety deposit box holding thirty-eight million Swiss francs in bearer bonds.

There were many plans to be made, and much work lay before me. But for the moment there was a bright sunny day coming up out of the south and east, spreading the broad central plains of Spain with warmth.

Maria was waiting for me when I returned. She had slept, she said, until just a few minutes before. Even the dogs came to greet me, wagging their tails. Koko licked my hand.

"Have you eaten?" She asked.

"*Sí*," I replied. "And you?"

"I am not hungry. I had coffee." She was absolutely at ease. She had redressed her wound, and through the half open door of the bathroom I could see things hanging on a string to dry.

"Have you slept, Monty?" She asked, staring at me. Her face was beginning to regain its color. She wore no makeup. Her nose shone, as did the hair that was pulled back around her ears. Her eyes were soft upon me.

"No," I said. "I would have stayed out today, but I better not go out in the daytime for some time yet."

"Then you must sleep." She stood and went to the bath. She pushed the drying things out of the way and began running a tub.

She came to the sill and stood leaning on the doorjamb. "Should I remain in the room?"

I did not want her to have to stay in the room while I slept." You would have to go without the dogs," I said. "They are too conspicuous."

"I know." She turned back to the tub and shut the water off. "There is no place I want to go. Your water is ready, Monty."

"What will you do all day while I sleep?"

She shrugged. "Your shirt needs to be washed. And I can borrow an iron from the manager's wife to press your suit."

"Is that what you want to do?"

"Your bath is ready," she said a second time. "The water was hot this morning. We are lucky it is still hot."

I stepped into the tub. She picked up a cloth, soaped it and began scrubbing my back. She worked slowly, carefully, softly. She sang a song in Spanish that told a story of a little bird at had broken its win and had been found by a virgin maid. She helped the bird fly again and when it was well, it turned into a prince and married the maid. They lived happily ever after in a grand palace that stood near the sea.

She pulled down the shades in the room while I rubbed myself dry. I could see her in the dim light, nude, waiting for me, hands at her sides. She was still singing the little song and sang until I stopped her with a kiss.

There was freedom now. The first blood rush in the cave in the mountains had passed. She was unafraid, she was with me. She moaned and tugged at my mouth with her own. She arched her back against me and whispered over and over in my ear. "Dear one! My darling!"

The lightness of her fingers, the urging of her body against me, the spasm of hunger that ran through her, were all at once and at the same time the pressures of love and the demands of desire.

We sank to the bed.

We loved.

Outside the window Madrid pounded its own way toward a bright high noon.

Chapter Twelve

A MAN LIKE Eustaquio Benedicto does not leave the key to his safety deposit box laying around. If the box contains thirty-eight million Swiss franc bearer bonds, it is likely that he carries it on his person—if he is a man like Eustaquio Benedicto.

And there was only one way to get the bonds. With the key. To plan a robbery with guns, scooping up the cash from the teller's cages is one thing. It can be plotted, charted and graphed into perfection. But to loot a safety deposit box—a specific box the number of which I did not know and would not know until I had seen the key—was quite another thing.

But there was a way, the only way that I could see where there was a chance of it working. I soon learned that Benedicto had no relatives. He was not married. He was not even sure where he had been born.

There was no one to hold as hostage and threaten him with. It would do no good to grab Benedicto himself. And to walk into the bank with the key to the box would be senseless.

But there was a way.

"How well are the dogs trained," I asked Maria that night.

"What do you want them to do?"

"Which is the smartest?"

"Rouge is the quickest to learn. But Koko is the steadiest. Perhaps it is because she is female. She will sit for hours without moving. Rouge will whine and grow very nervous after the first six or seven hours." She said. "Also Koko would be the easiest to teach to protect you. Rouge is the youngest and closer to me. I doubt he would divide his loyalty. I would say Koko. But what is your plan?"

"Then it will be Koko," I said. I called the animal over to me and fondled her ears. She licked my hand. "I am going to become a blind beggar on the streets of Madrid. Koko is going to lead me."

"I don't understand," she said.

"I will tell you what to do, my dear, when the time comes."

She nodded. "As you wish. When will you start working with the dog?"

"Tonight. At once. There isn't much time."

"How will we do that?"

"Leave Rouge here in the room. You and I will take a walk. At the first drugstore I will get a pair of dark glasses. First few nights we will walk her without a harness until I can make one."

"How will you do that?"

I turned in the room. "Coat hangers." I picked up her bag. "And several of these will give me enough leather to cover it. It will make a perfect harness."

Rouge did not like being left alone in the room but a sharp word from Maria and he settled down beside the bed. We left the hotel and were lucky no one saw us. I knew it would create a stir and comment if we took only the one dog out for a walk in the evening, but I did not want Rouge around while trying to train Koko to take me across streets and learn to read traffic.

We bought glasses, and at the shop further down the street Maria bought two large, roomy, soft leather handbags that would bind the coat hangers when I had worked them into a harness.

Once around the corner, I put the glasses on. "Give me the leash," I said.

She placed it in my hand. "I'm going to close my eyes." I said. "Talk to her. When we approach a curbing, tell her to stop and look for cars, for traffic. Speak softly to her."

"Why do you close your eyes?"

"To learn how a blind person walks. At best, their manner is uncertain, afraid. The braves of them, poor devils, are a little afraid. Have you ever noticed they never walk upright? Not really straight, upright? That is because they are cocking their heads forwards just a little, to hear, to feel what is ahead of them and around them. First I must walk with my eyes closed. I must learn to walk like the blind, and then I must remember how I walked so that later I can open my eyes behind the glasses and still give the illusion of being blind."

She listened patiently. "Very well, Monty," she said. "Are you ready?"

We were a dozen blocks away from the hotel. I slipped the glasses over my eyes and closed them. Immediately the noise of the street, horns, exhausts, snatches of conversations came to me alive and clear. I started to walk.

I nearly fell at the first curbing. At the second Koko stepped off into traffic and Maria jerked her back in time as a car sped past.

We continued. My back began to ache and I realized that I was straining forwards, without actually being aware of leaning forward. I wanted to open my eyes, but I did not dare. I continued until I had correctly analyzed the body position that was bringing on the ache and particular spot where it would ache.

Koko was beginning to respond well to Maria's soft encouragements by the time we started back to the hotel. It was not going to be easy. Just before I came to the place where we would stop our practice, I realized I had been shuffling. Not picking up my feet high enough to clear the ground.

Maria was tired, but I insisted that we take another turn of a few blocks until I had memorized the shuffle. And during this second turn I discovered that I was depending more and more on the dog. Koko had learned to stop at the curbing in one night.

I cannot fully describe my feeling when I took off the glasses and opened my eyes. I knew that it must be close to midnight. But it seemed that the sun was out.

We returned to the hotel exhausted and ready for sleep.

"Do we go again tomorrow night, Monty?" She asked, coming to me in the darkness, arms outstretched, bringing to me all of her loveliness and slim delicate beauty.

"Sì. Again tomorrow night until both Koko and I are as one. And I would fool the devil himself."

"Are you tired?"

"Very."

"Come to bed then." She drew me to her.

***

During the daylight hours of the next few days I took several dozen coat hangers and worked them, slowly, twisting, turning , into a harness for Koko. I then covered it with a plaiting of leather from the hand bags cut into strips. It was a neat job and fit the dog well. During the nights we had continued working on the leash and both Koko and I began to get the pattern of it. On the fourth night I worked with her using the harness. It was a complete success. The dog was sensitive and Maria carried a pocketful of tidbits to feed Koko every time she did something particularly well. I still worked with my eyes closed. And I had developed a hard core of posture that I knew I would never forget. I began to learn, too, the sudden sharpening of senses.

In a week there was little left for me to learn. I did not have to know all of the habits of a big city and the dog did not have to learn much. But it was enough. I was satisfied. On the last night, Koko and I went out alone, with Maria following a block behind us and across the street. We wandered throughout the city for hours and never once did the dog fail me. Maria caught up with us.

"It is wonderful!" She said. "Both of you look so *simpático*, it makes me want to cry."

That night we celebrated by dining out in a restaurant. It was the first meal we had taken outside of the hotel. Maria was radiant and full of life. We gave Koko a piece of bloody beef and did not forget to take one to Rouge. Maria got a little drunk and began to talk.

"She lived a very short time after I was born," she said, speaking of her mother. "I was raised by an aunt while Papa was there —he was going to school, he said—"

"Keep talking!" I said, my voice low. "Turn your head to the wall."

Estuardo walked into the café. I spoke to Koko and the dog picked up her beef and crawled under the table. The big man walked past the table and into the back of the room. He went through a door.

"Do you think he saw us?" I asked.

She shook her head. "I don't think so. But why—why do you wish to hide?"

"Let's go out of here." I said. I threw money onto the table and called Koko. We walked out into the street.

Two men got out of a car parked at the curb. I knew neither of them. But there was no mistake about their intentions. Both held their hands inside their pockets.

They were not hesitating. They meant business. On the left of Maria there was a row of flower boxes, the dried and crusted stems of long dead flowers sticking up out of twelve inches of soil.

The first one made a movement with his arm. I did not want to see what he was going to come out with. I shoved Maria across the flower boxes and dropped to one knee. I let him have two from the .45 and he was slammed back against the second who had gotten his gun hand free. His first shot was deflected into the sky. He didn't get a second chance.

Then I saw Koko move. As the dog had attacked me that night long ago in Paris, the bitch was down low and moving fast. She snarled and threw herself a good ten feet, whistling past my head and landing on something in back of me.

I spun around. Estuardo was down on his back, Koko at his throat.

I yanked at the harness and jerked the dog off. "No—No, Koko!" I yelled. She tore at the harness with frenzy trying to get at him. Estuardo made a bad mistake. He tried to bring up his Luger.

"Monty—No!" Maria screamed.

I heard her but it was too late. I let him have it quick and he never knew what hit him right between the eyes.

"Let's get out of here," I said, whistling for Koko and grabbing Maria. I shoved her into the car at the curb—Estuardo's car. The motor was still running. I shot it in gear and roared away.

The .45 U.S. Army Automatic is the most powerful hand weapon in the world. But it is an inanimate thing. The death of a man with a slug from my .45 in him is caused by me, and my forefinger, not by the gun. By me and my forefinger. The gun was still warm against my stomach.

It made five now. Two in Antwerp and three in Madrid. Five to one. The odds on Monty Nash were running out.

Five to one.

The woman was crying. The dog lunged excitedly from one side of the back seat to the other. The man driving the car was feeling a little of what they both felt. I wanted to cry. I wanted to lunge back and forth crazily. I wanted to get the hell out of all of it and go back to Cleveland.

But I wouldn't do that. I was being self-righteous. I was being what I was supposed to be. A tough sonofabitch who held tough opinions.

But it was still a crummy world and that was the way it remained for three days while I sat and listened to Maria cry in the hotel room.

The papers played it up big. They said it was gangsterism. But nobody believe that. Not in Madrid. They didn't know exactly what political faction had slaughtered the other. They didn't much care. Madrid is the most politically cynical capitol in the world. But one thing they did not believe — firmly — surely — was that it was gansterism.

Everyone in the hotel Granada had ideas about what had happened. And for three days I listened and tried to sell them worn-out machinery in between their speculations. I called numbers picked at random out of the telephone book and described the machinery in detail. It was supposed to be worn-out machine tools, and, while the hotel operator called me a fool for not calling on my customers in person and wasting my money on telephone calls, she sympathized with me for having a sick wife.

Once I even made a sale. But I called back and raised the price and the man called me an idiot.

That was all right too. I didn't mind. I didn't mind anything. I had three U.S. Army .45 Automatic pistols and spare rounds. I was tough. Three-Gun Monty, they called me on the West Side. And I'd never be taken alive.

Balls.

"Yes," I said to Koko and Rouge. "Balls."

On the fourth day Maria stopped crying and we went out in the night again to run some more tests on Koko and me. For six hours the dog and I were letter perfect, working together like a well-oiled machine.

The next morning Koko and I went out alone. I did not tell Maria what my plans were yet. There was time for that. She had not talked yet. She had not explained the three days of tears.

That's what I thought about as I stepped out of the alley were I had slipped on the dark glasses and pulled on the shabby overcoat and hat. I held the cigar box full of shoe laces in my left hand. With my right I held to the harness.

It was broad day light. And I had my eyes open.

I hadn't gone ten feet when someone dropped a coin in the box and walked on. The dog behaved beautifully. And the people of the streets behaved just as beautifully. Several times I had to empty the money into my pocket because of the weight on the box.

This, I said to myself, is not a bad way to make it.

Is it? Balls, I replied. Don't make fun, boy—just don't.

Maria was smiling when I returned.

The next day there was a freezing rain, but I went out anyway. I was soaked through the skimpy coat in an hour and the rest of the day I spent shuddering, teeth popping, fighting against the penetrating winds and the rain. Naturally I caught a cold and I had to remain in the hotel for two days. But it was a weekend and I did not mind. I also did not mind having Maria to take care of me.

I even got used to having Koko sleep with me. But I didn't mind. Not after what she had done to save my life.

After the first three days, nothing more was mentioned in the papers about the "gangsterism." Maria did not mention it again either. Not until I asked her about it.

"Why the tears?" I asked in between sneezes. I intentionally made my voice a little harsh. "You don't seem the type."

"Don't be cruel, Monty," she said to me.

"Don't mean to be. But—you must admit that it was strange behavior. For one who is bound to the oath."

She did not look at me. She watched the continuing rain in the streets below our window. "Estuardo was my brother."

Chapter Thirteen

I NEVER FULLY REALIZED, until that moment, what depth there was to the fanaticism in the medallion society. I had seen Helga de Loon commit suicide, but there was a great deal of cynical weariness in her gesture. She had been through a war. She had suffered greatly. She had bloody years of living in a sick world piled up behind her. She could have believed the promise of death in the oath of the medallion carriers and taken her own life because of that fear. She could have bitten into the capsule just because of weariness.

In Duval and the others I had come into contact with in the mountains near Cuneo I had seen only a group of men using a device. The disc was a way of life for them. They would, I had no doubt, someday drop out of sight, or cleverly arrange their own deaths to avoid persecution by the society, and take off for the bushes in South America or somewhere else with a suitcase full of loot—forgetting the medallion society. In Maria I saw only a young girl of breath-taking beauty who was dedicated to the society. But *only* to the society. There had not been one word or gesture in our relationship to suggest that she was a politically aware person, or that her motive for being a medallion carrier was anything other than something her father had been, or her brother and Anton, whom she had described as her closest friend.

Political fanatics are never quiet. They wear their opinions and views on their breastplates and they pound them with a infuriated fist, crying *against*, never *for*, something.

If she had not heart for the society, why then was she in it? For the romance? The adventure? There was no adventure in the way we were living or romance in the threat of death coming down on us at any movement that was not just right.

It hit me like an electric shock. Fear!

Of what?

Death, kiddo. *Death.*

"Was Estuardo sent here to kill us—you—me?"

"Both of us."

"How do you know?"

"The two men you killed on the sidewalk—" She shuddered. "They are assassins."

"How would you know that?"

She could not look at me. "I have worked with them before. In Rome."

"You fingered a job for them?"

"Yes."

"Then where is the percentage in working for the society," I said cautiously, with just the slightest edge of harshness in my voice, "if one may be killed at any moment—and by one's own brother?"

It was a rough thing to do to her. She had already gone through it for three days, probably asking herself the same question.

"There is no escape. One obeys."

She then turned on me. "You are not a true member of the medallions, are you, Monty?"

"Yes." I said. "I am a member."

"I don't believe you," she replied.

"I am a true member," I said, trying to get all of the honest conviction I could into my voice.

"No. You are lying."

"What makes you think so?"

"You wanted to know the percentage of working for a society that may kill you at any moment—even by one's own brother."

I bit my lip. She was right in there. It had been a slip. Monty Nash is not superhuman. Monty Nash made a slip. I waited.

"That is not enough to convict a man with, Maria." I said.

"*Sí*, it is enough for the society."

"You truly believe me to be lying?"

"Truly."

"What now?"

"I don't know," she said. "If you are an enemy agent, my life may be in danger."

100

"It is not."

"How can I believe you?"

"That is true," I said.

"There is one thing."

"What?"

"Do you love me?"

I replied instantly. Only a moment later did I realize that I was speaking half truth—half lie. "Yes, Maria. I love you."

"Will you marry me?"

"Yes."

"Today?"

"Yes."

"Would you have married me—later?"

I didn't answer.

She paced the room several times and stopped before me. "I cannot help you. I know nothing about the society but that I take orders from Duval and Anton. I do not know how many of us there are, who they are, where they are. I know that in Rome there is a meeting place like that in the Italian mountains near the village that is outside Cuneo."

"I did not ask you that," I said.

"I know—I know." Her voice was a little desperate. "But whatever you are, I want to tell you everything."

"Why?"

"Love is the door to the soul."

"And to the gates of hell."

"Yes."

"Don't tell me any more." I stood and walked to the window. "I don't want to know any more. I am on a mission. There are things that I must do."

"But why go on when you must know they will kill you if they get the chance?"

"And if I do not go on?" I asked.

"Also—death," she said.

***

That night when my cold had subsided a bit, we lay side by side. She held my hand, and brought it up slowly to her lips and pressed it against her cheek.

"Are you a brave man, Monty?"

"Yes," I said.

"Let me hear you say it—fully."

"I am a brave man."

"Then take me with you to some country and let us live."

"No," I said.

I don't know when she went to sleep. But I was awake most of the night listening to her breathing.

Everything taught to me as an agent was being violated. And finally I had committed the cardinal sin. I had become emotionally involved with the enemy.

Like Orrick. He had had sympathy for me and I had escaped.

Like Orrick, I was letting myself become wide open for deviation from the straight, strict rules of the pursuit. She had already made a demand. To leave everything and go to another country. To marry her.

I began to cough. She awoke. She made me tea and laced it heavily with Spanish brandy. I drank it. We didn't talk. There seemed to be nothing left to say. She had sensed that I was not a medallion carrier. But she did not know for sure. She knew that I was much taken with her, but she didn't know how deeply.

I didn't know myself.

She turned out the light. She came to me, putting her head on my shoulder. "I have a cold." I said.

"I know." She kissed me.

It was lovemaking at ten thousand pounds of pressure per square inch; it was lovemaking at crazy speeds and dizzying heights. There was a little torment, more than a little pain and the greatest of joys.

102

She slept, exhausted, finally, while I smoked. It was growing light outside.

"Maria?" I said gently. She did not respond.

"Maria?"

I got up quietly and dressed, pressing my nostrils together to keep from sneezing.

The dogs stirred. Koko came to my side, licked my hand and then went to get her harness. I hesitated. After all, I had not told Maria of my plan. I stopped quickly and slipped the harness on Koko's shoulders and around her neck. Rouge looked on, unhappy that he was not going with us.

I was dressed. I drank a quick shot of brandy and stepped to the side of the bed. I slipped down beside her and kissed her lightly on the cheek.

That was all. That was good-bye. I stood, took all the money and the three forty-fives and the spare clips. I opened the door and Koko followed. I closed the door softly behind me.

I hit the street and walked clear across Madrid, sneezing most of the way, found a cheap hotel and checked in. There was some argument about Koko, but a little extra under the table seemed to please the hard-eyed man at the desk.

I bought a bottle of brandy and a dozen oranges and piled the blankets and everything else I could get, including Koko, onto the bed and got in.

It was a nasty thirty-six hours, and I'm not sure whether I was just plain drunk or half out of my mind with the cold, but it broke after a session of eight hours straight sweating. It took me another day to regain my strength and by that time the weather had cleared a little.

I bought secondhand clothes and found a secluded alley where I could change my outer coat while Koko stood guard. I emerged as a blind man with a large dog. I worked my way through the streets and stopped before the building across the street from the bank.

Nothing happened, except that I got tired of standing still and trying to keep Koko from growling at everyone who stopped to drop a coin into my cigar box.

That night I left the hotel without Koko and bought some hair dye—six bottles of it. The nest morning, Koko was a black dog with hair as shiny as the finest of the señoritas who dropped a coin in my box. The second day I met the cop on the beat. The third he talked to me for five minutes. The fourth day he stopped and chatted for nearly an hour.

I debated on whether I should go out on Saturday and reasoned that it would be the best day for a blind man selling pencils. I returned to my spot across the street from the bank.

I watched every movement that occurred across the street. Nothing outward was suspicious. I saw no one that I thought might be a medallion carrier. I saw nothing suspicious about the dress shop. I talked to a merchant from Barcelona for a half hour who tried to sell me a rug to stand on, and I talked to the cop. That night I bought Koko a beef steak. And that night I called Maria.

"I'm sorry I had to leave so suddenly. Is everything all right?"

"*Sí*. Where are you?"

"Setting something up," I said. "I couldn't get in touch with you before this."

"Should I stay and wait for you to call?" She sounded as if nothing had happened.

"Yes. I hate to keep you in that room, but you should be there should I need anything."

"But the dog—"

"Take him out at night. I won't call you late at night." I said. "I have to go now, Maria."

"*Sí*." There was a catch in her voice. "I miss you."

"And I love you," I said, gritting my teeth. "I must go. Good-by darling. And stay in the room."

"*Sí*. Good-by."

***

I spent Sunday working up a basic plan. I knew the movements of the people who worked inside the bank now, when they arrived and how. I knew about the man and women who operated the dress shop. I knew about the cop who talked to me. In a week I had become a fixture on the street.

It was time to think about Benedicto. And I had a way of doing that too. I left the hotel and entered the nearest café, found the telephone book and looked up Juan Banigo, manager of the bank. He lived in an apartment building on the southern side of Madrid, and it was a pleasant ride for a sunny Sunday afternoon.

I found the apartment building and entered, rode to his floor and rang his bell. I slipped a handkerchief western style across my face, pulled out a .45, reversed it and waited. The door cracked. I lunged into it, slammed him against the wall and chopped him in the back of the head. He sank to the floor.

I closed the door and searched the apartment quickly, found it empty and relaxed. I went to the phone and called Benedicto at his ranch, where I knew he would be on a Sunday afternoon—looking at his bulls, drinking tall drinks and dreaming about his past while dallying with the present and shrugging off the future.

Or at least I hoped he would be there on a sunny Sunday afternoon. It really made little difference as long as someone answered telephone.

I got Benedicto on the first try. "Señor? This is Juan Banigo, manager of the bank—"

"The bank?" His voice was full of alarm. "Who is it?"

"Juan Banigo, señor—" I waited.

"Ah, sí. Señor Banigo. How are you?"

"What was that, señor?" I held the phone away from my face at arm's length, hardly speaking above a whisper. "We have a bad line, señor. I must speak with you—"

"What was that? I can't hear you. Speak up. What is the matter?"

"A bad connection—call me back señor, if you please. Do you have my number—"

"Your number—yes. I will get it—"

I hung up. I sat still, lit a cigarette and watched the man on the floor lie very still. Benedicto called back in exactly two minutes and forty-three seconds.

"Ah—that is better, señor—tell me, how are the bulls—"

"What do you want, señor?" His voice was hard. He didn't want to talk about bulls. He wanted to know what the hell was going on.

"Señor, I thought I might warn you. There have been—er, ah—certain irregularities showing up in your accounts. I thought I would speak to you—er, ah—before there was an official question raised at the bank."

"What kind of irregularities?"

"A shortage, señor. A very large shortage. When, may I ask, was the last time you withdrew—a hundred thousand pesetas?"

"What?" It was the cry of a wounded bull. "I have never drawn such an amount—"

I cut in immediately. "Just as I thought, señor. Then I was right in approaching you unofficially. There is a thief in the bank señor." I made my voice as sad and as soothing as possible. "But you need not fear. We are fully covered by insurance against embezzlements. But if you could come down in the morning with your books, a little before the bank opens, we might go over this thing in quiet. We may be able to spring a trap and catch the thief."

"Of course—of course. I fully understand, señor." He was nervous as a June bride. "So good of you to think of my—interest. I shall be there."

"At eight?" I suggested. "With all of your records?"

"At eight."

"And perhaps, Señor Benedicto, it would be wise to check the contents of your safety deposit box as well."

"You are absolutely right. Of course. At eight. And a thousand thanks, señor. I will remember your thoughtfulness."

"Good-by."

I waited. It took him ten minutes to decide to call again, just to make sure. His voice was wary. "How much do you think is missing?" He asked cagily.

"There is no way of knowing, señor." I said. "But we will know at once when I see your own records."

"Very well."

He hung up again. I stood, looked at Banigo and began to strip the room. I robbed him of some five thousand pesetas, a beautiful gold wrist watch and a stick pin. Then I slipped out of the door.

*****

In the morning, at seven-thirty, I was on the street with Koko. The car I had stolen and parked half a block away from the bank during the night had not been touched. At seven-thirty-five it began to rain heavily.

I patted the dog on the head and pulled her close to the wall and out of the rain as much as possible. I searched the street. It was empty. Nothing moved.

I went over Toro's floor plan in my mind, working out the distances again and again as I had done in my hotel room. There was no detail inside the bank that the artist had left out. I knew the bank as well as if I had been inside myself a dozen times.

At seven-forty I began to search for the man and woman who ran the dress shop. They would be the first.

Seven-forty-five. Nothing moved. There was no one in the streets. I began to get nervous. What if Banigo had gotten the bright idea that he hadn't just been robbed? That perhaps there was something else behind my attack on him? And what if Benedicto decided to call again—and learned of my attack?

Seven-forty-eight. Nothing.

I loosened the .45 in my right-hand pocket and took a firm grip on the dog's harness.

Seven-fifty. The dress shop owners had not shown up yet.

Something was wrong!

Had they been warned to stay away? True, it was raining and they could be delayed in a dozen ways.

I began to sneeze again. Koko looked up at me questioningly. I patted her on the head. "Takes a good man to crack a bank single-handed, doesn't it, Koko. But I wouldn't be single-handed, would I? I'd have you."

She licked my fingers and whined. She sat, and then she stood.

My hand froze on the harness. Two men were coming down the street. They wore black raincoats and their heads were bent against the rain and the wind. They were not regulars on the street, not workers in any of the shops. But there was something familiar about them. Something that was either cop—or goon. They passed the bank without looking at it.

"What would people like that be doing out—walking—on a day like this, Koko?"

I got no answer. They were past the bank and at the dress shop. They wheeled inside, opened the door with a key and stepped in.

I didn't know what it meant. And I was getting another cold, and I didn't much care. "All bets are off, Koko." I said, taking a firm grip of her harness in one hand and the butt of the .45 in the other. "We're going to have to wing it from here."

She stood up, alert. "Let's go buy a dress, Koko, baby."

We crossed the street and walked right up to the dress shop door and opened it. I was inside before they knew I was there.

One of them had taken off his jacket. His shoulder holster was tight. I waved a gun in their faces. "Rainy outside, ain't it?" I said.

One of them tried for his gun. "Koko!" I said. The dog had been trained for quick movements. I saw her teeth sink into the man's forearm. He went down. The other man tried to use the cover for a chance at his arm holster. I let him have it in the heart. The slug went clear through him and shattered a glass case in back of the shop. There was blood all over the carpeting.

"Señor—please—señor—" The second fought Koko and begged me at the same time.

"Koko!" She let go of him. And he sank to the floor looking at his companion and then up at me.

"What are you doing here?" I asked.

He bit his lip so hard his teeth went through. I distinctly remember laughing. It was that kind of mood. I tore at my collar again and threw the coat to one side. I was sweating now.

"You going to talk, señor?"

He looked fearfully at the dog. "Señor—what will happen to me?"

"Tell me the truth and I'll have to decide."

"We were to wait here for you. We knew that you would be coming."

"How did you know?"

"We received orders from Duval in Paris."

"To kill me on sight?"

"*Sí.*"

"And when Estuardo failed, you decided to cover the bank."

"On orders, señor."

"What did you think I would do? Walk into the front door and try to force the vault?"

"We did not know what you would do, señor. We just had our orders."

"Do you carry the medallion, señor?" I asked.

"*Sí.*"

"Where are the owners of this shop?"

Koko answered that for me. She had gone off to investigate. She whined and jumped back. I stepped to the back room leaving Koko to guard the man on the floor.

There were two of them. A man and a woman. They had been dead about two days.

It was a crazy world. A sick, mad, crazy world and I was the craziest of them all. I went back to him.

"What is your name, señor?"

"José."

"All right, José, you tell me something. Is there a back door to the bank?"

"*Sí.*"

"Do they ever open it?"

"The cleaning women are in there now. They always come an hour earlier and then take the trash out of the back way. There is an alley that runs along the back of the whole block."

I left Koko to watch him and went to the back of the shop. I opened the back door and looked out. There was a high fence separating the dress shop rear from the bank rear. I piled several boxes on top of one another and looked over. There was a back door—and it was open.

I went back into the shop. "When will the cleaning women clean up and get out?"

"They leave when the bank is opened for business."

"You're sure?"

"*Sí, señor*. I would have no reason to lie."

Not much, I thought, if you carried the medallion. "Is there anyone inside the bank with the cleaning women?"

I watched his eyes. They told me everything. There was someone inside the bank with the cleaning women—a night watchman to let them in. No cleaning woman in the world would have the key to a bank. The guard let them in every morning. Any move against the back door would probably mean four alarms in four different directions and a load of buckshot—or worse.

"There is no one inside the bank, señor," he said, "but the women."

I then told him why I thought he was lying. He thought I was going to kill him and I nearly did when I hit him on the head with the butt of the gun. I tied him up and pulled him out of the way.

I had to work fast now. I sneezed. Then I began to cough.

In a few minutes I had to have a plan.

The street outside was quiet. Nothing but the steady rain.

What had happened that would prevent me from going through with my original idea?

Nothing that hadn't been taken care of. The only unusual event in the routine of the morning had been the arrival of the two medallion carriers.

"Koko!" The dog came to my side. I took a deep breath and stepped outside into the rain.

I moved to the front of the bank and stood just inside, waiting for Señor Benedicto.

I didn't have to wait long.

110

Chapter Fourteen

BENEDICTO arrived in a three-year-old American Cadillac, parked in front of the bank and dashed for the door.

"Koko!" I said softly.

The dog leaped. Benedicto stopped. I then went into my act. I began to shuffle around wildly, calling the dog. "Koko—Koko—come back here, you bad girl!"

Benedicto stopped just inside the doorway. "It is all right, señor," he said. He patted the dog, took her harness and walked to my side. He reached for my hand to place the harness in my palm and I stepped in close, back to the glass door of the bank, and slipped the .45 out and into his side. "Stand very still, Señor Benedicto and do not move or speak unless I tell you to."

"Wha—"

"Señor!" I rammed the gun in his gut. "I am a very desperate man, señor, please."

"What are you doing—a blind man—"

"I am not blind, señor and I will not hesitate to shoot you down where you stand if you do not do as I say!"

He relaxed. He wasn't wild or nervous. He had been around, Benedicto had, he knew when a man had a .45 rammed into your stomach, you didn't try to escape.

"That's it," I coaxed. "Now just walk with me and stand at my side, as if we were talking and trying to stay out of the rain."

We moved to the side of the doorway.

"I don't know what your plan is, señor—"

"You will learn soon enough," I said. "Turn with your back to the door and face me. That's it," I said. "Now just stand still."

The gun was hidden from view of both the street and the inside of the bank. "What time is it?" I asked.

"Eight-thirty." He replied.

"We won't be much longer."

At a quarter to nine the first of the arrivals took place. A woman. One of the secretaries to the manager, if I could believe Toro's drawings and his descriptions of the people. He had not missed much of the detail. I recognized her instantly.

"Speak to her." I said softly. "Tell her you are waiting for Señor Banigo and ask her if you could step inside out of the rain."

She spoke to me first, a few kind words and a blessing. She dropped a coin when she saw I had no cigar box. She became flustered and begged my pardon. I stood rigid as though seeing nothing, but I thanked her for the blessing. I nudged Benedicto with the gun.

"I am expected by Señor Banigo, señorita," he said in a surprisingly courtly manner, "and I wonder if I might wait inside."

"Of course, Señor Benedicto," she replied. She rang the bell at the side of the door and waited. They passed the time of day and commented on the weather.

The guard came to the door and looked out. Seeing nothing alarming, he opened the door.

"Koko!" I said. The dog was inside and on the guard before he had opened the door a foot. I shoved Benedicto and the woman in before me and stepped to one side.

"There will be no bloodshed if everyone does as I tell them. Where are the cleaning women?" I asked the guard.

He indicated the lower room where the vault would be. I waved them all down the stairs. I had the guard tie them all and stretch them out, face down on the floor. Then I took him back upstairs to the main floor.

We just made it as two men, tellers, came to the door. They offered no resistance and without a word did as they were told. The guard tied them up.

Eight minutes to nine. The time lock on the vault should be turned off at three minutes to nine. The manager, the assistant manager and two more employees, a teller and another secretary, had to show up.

I left Koko in the vault basement and told all of them that the dog was trained to attack if they made a noise or tried to move. They believed me. They had not made a sound and they had not moved an inch when I came down with the last secretary and teller.

That left only Señor Banigo and the assistant manager.

At least five minutes to nine they arrived together. Banigo's head was bandaged. He was talking rapidly to the assistant and touching his head, explaining no doubt what had happened the day before.

He tried to shout and break for the door and the street when he saw me, but he slipped on the wet, water-slicked floor and went down. I hit him over the head and turned to the assistant manager, a hard-faced little man, probably a Swiss national, with thin lips and his love for money expressed in every line of his face.

"You had better know how to open the vault, señor," I said.

"I do—señor," he said, shaking with fear.

"Let's go."

Everyone but the manager, who was still unconscious on the floor, was made to put their noses down and keep them down. At three minutes to nine, the assistant manager flipped the switch, which cut off the alarm, and stepped to the face of the vault.

"There are double dials, señor—"

"What is the combination for the other dial?" I demanded. The two dials were five feet apart. Both of them had to be operated at the same time. One man could not open the vault.

He was not supposed to know the combination of the second dial. He glanced fleetingly at the others on the floor, then gave me the readings.

"Begin," I said.

We began to work the dials and in a moment the great door was unlocked and open. He turned on the light.

An inner vault where the bank would hold cash and bank securities lay ahead. He started for it. On either side were the safety deposit boxes.

"This is far as we go," I said. "Stand still."

He stood still. I went back to Benedicto. "Señor," I said, bending down beside him, "I want the key to the safety deposit box." I placed the gun at the back of his head. "And I want it now."

He didn't hesitate a second. "Around my neck."

I found the chain, rifled it around his neck and jerked it free. "You—" I stepped back into the vault and spoke to the assistant manager— "the other key."

"But, señor—the money—the securities are in the inner vault—"

"Your key!" I demanded.

"Sí, señor." He came forward and pulled out a key ring. Moving very slowly and showing me that he was moving slowly, he selected one. "Four-twenty-one—" I said.

We opened the door and I slipped the long, flat box out. There were two envelopes. One held personal papers, and the second thirty-eight sheets of neatly folded bond paper. These were certificates of one million Swiss francs each, bearer demand.

I shoved them into my pocket.

No one had moved. They were in exactly the same positions as I had left them. Koko wagged her tail as I retreated out of the vault.

Just as I turned back to the stairs leading to the upper floor I saw the assistant manager busy with the vault holding the cash and securities of the bank. Why not, Mac, I thought. You'll probably never be able to explain how you knew the combination of the second dial anyway. Good luck.

I went around the upper stairs and into the main floor. I headed for the back, made the still open rear door and scaled the fence after heaving the dog over.

Inside the dress shop again, nothing had changed. I removed my coat and hat and pulled on the coat of the owner of the dress shop, who stared at me dead-eyed.

I was dressed and ready to leave the shop when I heard the alarm go off in the bank. "Koko!" I said.

We left through the front door and walked slowly past the front of the bank. Then we got into the car I had stolen in Vallecas.

They hadn't even opened the front door of the bank when I turned the corner and drove off into the thickening rain.

I left the car near the Prado and walked over two blocks and caught a cab. I ordered the driver to drive down the street where the Granada Hotel was located.

I got out and told him to wait. Koko recognized the street and began to jerk at the least to get away. I said good-by to her and let her go. She raced through the rain toward the hotel. My only fear for the dog was that Maria would not be there. But every man with a dog in Spain would be suspect for the next week. I had to let her go.

"I'll go to the Prado," I said to the driver.

I sneezed and coughed for the whole ride. I got out and took another cab. I rode to the opposite side of Madrid and took another cab to Vallecas. In Vallecas I stopped in a drugstore and bought some aspirin and, at a small café next door, a small bottle of brandy.

Outside in the street I waited for a bus, sneezing and fighting off a rising flush in my head. The bus clambered up and I climbed aboard wearily. "Railroad station," I said.

I paid my fare and found a seat in the rear of the bus. I closed my eyes and only then became aware of the tightness in my stomach. It seemed as though it had been tight all my life.

I thought about Maria.

It was not easy to think of her. But deep inside of me I knew I was one hundred per cent right. What the hell did I have to do with a sick world that was going to hell with itself? Would what I was doing, had done, would do, materially affect the decisions that would be made by an anthill of men on whether the world would be blown up or not? Did it? Did it? I pressed that one into my hard head and locked it there. I had to make myself believe that what I was doing was important. And *would* affect those decisions made in a gloomy room in a gloomy palace by half-mad men imagining themselves to be the saviors of the world.

I thought more of Maria. Of her body. Of the night in the mountains—

She had made sense. She had said let's get the hell away from it now that we've found something.

It was beautiful—so simple. Forget Cleveland, London, Paul Austin, forget everything and go away with her. To hell with them—both sides. *Both sides*. That was the key.

Like Orrick, something had gotten to me. But unlike Orrick I hoped to avoid what might happen because of it.

I had run because they were zeroing in on me from two sides. I had not the slightest doubt that there would be others, and there had been—in the dress shop. And I had no doubt that Orrick and Sheldon would be combing the town for me. Perhaps by now there were others sent in by Rex and GloSec Europe.

I had run because of Maria. Because, in spite of believing that she had loved me, or the possibility of my loving her, she had fingered me to Estuardo and the other two. And she would again.

She had picked out the café where Estuardo had moved against me.

There was only one question nagging me. Why did they want me knocked off? Even if they suspected me, why not let me go and try to lift the bonds—

But suddenly I did realize the reason for the two in the dress shop. They were supposed to get me on the way out of the bank—and get the bonds, too.

I took a slug of brandy and half a dozen aspirin, and clambered down from the bus. I went aboard the train and sat down. And I was still seated comfortably when an hour later the train came in to Aranjuez—one of the most beautiful cities in Spain. But I didn't see much.

For two reasons.

It was still raining. And I was drunk from brandy and a rapidly rising fever.

Aspirin—brandy—sneeze—curse—and dream about Maria. In that order. It went like that all the away to Valencia.

116

Chapter Fifteen

I ARRIVED in Valencia in need of two things. A place to hide and someone to take care of me. I knew that it wasn't going to be long before I would fall flat on my face. The fever that I had been fighting off finally blew its top and my breath was becoming labored.

The good brothers of the *monasterio* San Juan Bautista solved both of my problems. I stayed in their infirmary for four days. When I re-emerged into the sun flecked streets of Spain's resort city on the Mediterranean the press was still carrying accounts of the robbery on their front pages. But it was not as important as it had been. It was only a matter of time, the press stated, before the second man would be caught—as soon as the Madrid police made the assistant manager reveal the name and whereabouts of his accomplice.

They had caught him before he got out of Madrid with a suitcase full of cash.

I sent the brothers de San Juan Bautista a thousand Swiss francs.

That night I caught a train for Barcelona and went immediately to the bus station to catch a bus to Ripoll. I arrived in the sleepy mountain community at dawn and started out at once for the border. That night I slept in the hills and dreamed about Maria. And the next morning I began the long climb into the Pyrenees. By sundown that evening I was on my way to Prades, inside France. I then began to make my way back to Paris, going west to Bordeaux and taking the Paris express. I arrived in Paris near midnight and went immediately to the Café Alié in Makakoff.

***

Napoleon is said to have remarked that the element of surprise was the attacker's greatest single advantage during any conflict. This is a debatable remark. American Indians often came over the hill in total surprise to the wagon train moving west. Often they were bettered in the fight by superior forces and better marksmanship.

In my case I planned a direct assault on Duval and the medallion society. And I needed support. Not much support. Just someone I could trust.

André was surprised to see me. But there was more shock in his voice than the unexpectedness of my sudden appearance.

"*Mon ami!* What has happened to you? You look as if you had lost twenty-five pounds!"

"I probably have, monsieur."

"The way you left—leaving the money—there was no need to pay me for the old coat." He wagged his finger under my nose. "Where have you been? Have you found anything about the murderer of your friend?"

"Getting closer all the time, André," I said.

"Come, sit with me and talk." He retired to his stool beside the cashier's corner, and I sat in the chair beside him.

"Has there been anyone here looking for me?" I asked.

He hesitated just long enough, "*Oui.*"

"Americans?"

"*Oui.*"

"How often do they come?"

"Every night."

"*Bon,*" I said. I stood. "I want to use your back room for a while."

He looked at me queerly. "As you wish," he said.

I entered the back room. It was as if nothing had happened in between. There had been no Maria, no Duval, no Estuardo, no Madrid, no robbery.

I picked up the phone. I called Duval.

He answered. "Duval." He said.

"*Zurrapa,*" I said.

"Where are you?" He demanded at once.

"Not so fast, monsieur," I said quietly. "There are a few things I would like to know."

"Do not be insubordinate!" He said. "Where are you?"

"Why did Estuardo and the others try to kill me?"

118

"I know nothing of it. Will you stop this stupid talk and tell me where you are?"

"And the others in the dress shop next to the bank, monsieur. Who ordered them there to wait for me?"

He did not reply. "You are playing a joke," he said finally.

"Not at all, monsieur," I said. "Before I turn over the—er—Swiss documents to the society, I must know about these things."

"Do you know the penalty for refusing to obey an order?"

"Death," I said automatically.

"Exactly, monsieur. Now. At once, tell me where you are."

"I will come to you," I said. "What is your address?"

"You cannot come here. I cannot take the chance."

"I will contact you," I said. I hung up.

That would set them on fire. I went back to André. "Monsieur, I need several men I can trust for a certain bit of business."

"What kind of men, *mon ami?*"

"You were in the underground."

"*Oui.*"

"Men like that. But not Communist."

"For what purpose?"

"You might say that it will help France."

"I do not joke about such things lightly, monsieur." He fixed me with a cold eye. "Not lightly."

"You have my word."

"That may not be enough," he said.

"You are worried about the visiting Americans?"

When he didn't reply, I knew he was. I needed his help. I needed the kind of men he could give me. There was only one way to get this and that was by telling him the truth.

"I will wait for you in the back, then I will tell you anything you ask."

"That may be too late." He nodded toward the door. Tris Guardian and another agent I did not know were about to enter the Café Alié.

I turned and started for the back of the café. "Give me time to explain, André," I said over my shoulder. I didn't think they had seen me, but I wasn't going to wait around to find out. I went out the back way and doubled back to the front of the café. I watched them from across the street. They spoke to André and had a glass of cognac. They stayed about fifteen minutes. If he had told them anything they would have left right away. He hadn't said a word.

They left and I re-entered the café. He did not seem surprised to see me come in from the front.

"Merci, monsieur," I said and walked to the back.

He closed the café early that night and joined me in the back. He did not speak right away. He made a great show of being tired and getting himself into a comfortable position. When he turned to face me, he had a Luger in his hand."

"I must protect myself, monsieur," he said.

"Why?"

"They say things about you that are difficult to believe, but despite the difficulty, I must protect myself."

"What did they say?"

"That you are a traitor to your country."

"Do you believe that?"

"I do not know what to believe, monsieur."

"May I take something out of my pocket?"

"As long as it is not a gun."

I pulled out the thirty-eight million franc bonds. "Do you know what these are?"

He looked at them. He knew. His eyes told me that he knew.

"This is the cheese, monsieur, with which I will catch the biggest rat in Europe."

"Where did you get them?"

"Will you put down the gun?"

He put it down. I grinned. "You had the safety on, André. You've lost your touch."

He looked at the gun quickly. "*Sacre—*"

I laughed and put the bonds back in my pocket.

"André, there are those of us who see the world going to hell—"

He nodded. "Directly—straight—" He nodded again.

"Once before I have told a friend this story and he promised to help me. As it turned out, he did not."

"It depends on the story, *mon ami*," he said.

"Listen, then, André," I said, feeling some of the heat return to my voice. "What you fought in the underground was but child's play compared to what thousands of us are fighting now. And what we fight is not only in an occupied country. It's in all countries, in all cities of the world."

He waited.

"There is a society, André, that is more dedicated, more intelligent, more capable than the best of those who fought with you in the underground here during the occupation." I tossed him the medallion. "Unscrew it."

He did so. While he held the faded bits of red cloth, I told him everything.

When I was finished, and had explained why I was doing it, why the agents who came to his café called me a traitor, he replied at once.

"How many men do you want?"

"I will need two dozen."

"Two dozen!"

"*Oui*. And they must bring their own guns and be prepared to die. Some of them may well die, monsieur. But the cause is no less urgent or the reasons no less demanding than those for which they fought during the Nazi occupation."

"Two dozen. That will take time."

"How long?"

"A day."

121

"That is enough."

"What will I tell them they are going to do?"

"Fight for—freedom," I said. And somehow it did not come out corny.

"But the fight, monsieur. What will you have them do?"

"Invade Italy."

"Italy—invade Italy?"

"It is where they are, monsieur."

He nodded. "Tomorrow night at this time."

"Only those who can be trusted, monsieur. Those who are not Communist."

"*Oui.*"

***

A Swiss franc is worth, roughly, twenty-five cents. I had in my possession, in my pocket, roughly 9,500,000 dollars.

It was enough to entice the most stouthearted man of honor to try his hand at catching me. Duval would try. Others would be looking for me. In fact, without reading a newspaper, I knew that I was the object of a very desperate and intense search by the police, the members of the medallion society, and every crook, thief and would-be adventurer in Europe. But I was going to give Duval a little edge.

It took me nearly three hours to find out that Vosges 8-5980 was the telephone number of one Monsieur Paul de Seraic, and that he lived in one of the newer and shinier apartment buildings in what is known as the "inner ring" of the boulevards and avenues circling through the city.

I found a back entrance and, making sure there was an easy way to get in, left and walked the nearest avenue until I came to a telephone, only a block away. I called Duval.

"Monsieur de Seraic?" I asked before he could speak.

It stung him. "*Oui?*"

"This is a friend. Nash has called the police. You must leave at once."

"What—who is this . . . ?" I hung up.

I ran like hell back to the apartment building and entered through the rear. I waited for him to come out. He strode out of the building followed by three men. There was no doubt about who they were and what their function was.

As soon as they were out of sight I strode openly into the lobby. The doorman opened the door for me respectfully. I smiled, then stopped and snapped my fingers. *"Oh, pardon, monsieur!"*

"Oui, monsieur?"

"I forgot something—and I wouldn't want to return at this moment."

"Oui, monsieur?" He looked at me questioningly.

I winked at him knowingly. "My friend has a dinner guest, monsieur."

"Ahhh!" He understood. *"Ahh, oui."*

"I wonder if I might use your lobby phone to call him?"

"But of course, monsieur!" He replied, full of appreciation that I would not interrupt a man's games.

We walked back to the small alcove off the main lobby. I quickly stepped in front of him and picked up the receiver, pushing a button at random. I smiled at him and turned my back, depressing the receiver with my finger. "Jean!" I said into the dead phone. "Oh——I am so sorry. Yes, may I get my portfolio?"

The doorman was listening. I scanned the list of names.

"Oui. At once." I found de Seraic's name. 12-B.

I turned back to the doorman. "Nothing has happened yet."

"But it will, monsieur." He grinned at me. "It will."

"Of course," I said. I strode to the elevator. *"Merci, monsieur."*

He nodded with a broad grin on his face and returned to his place beside the front door. "Twelve," I said to the operator.

There wouldn't be much time. He would be waiting in a car nearby. When the police didn't show up in a few minutes he would come charging back inside.

I had no time to fool around with the lock. I kicked it open on the third try. No one came to their doors to find out what was going on. I don't know what I would have done if they had.

I stepped inside. I began to my right and searched everything, starting with the carpeting, pictures on the walls, stuffing in the chairs, a desk—everything. I worked my way around the living room and finally tore out the light fixtures. Then I started on the two bedrooms. I worked them the same way. It did not take me long. I had been taught how to search—and I had a lot of experience.

There was not one paper. Not one letter or one slip of anything— not even a laundry ticket. Duval was playing it the right way. He had everything with him—either in a briefcase, or in his head.

Duval struck me as the type that would do it both ways.

I left my calling card. I slipped one of the bonds out of the envelope and pinned it to the dangling light fixture in the middle of the living room with an ice pick.

Just before I got out of there I yanked the telephone out of the wall, then I made it to the fire stairs in a dead run. I had not tried to muffle the noise of my search. There were a few people standing in the doors looking toward Duval's apartment. One of them even tried to stop me. I kicked him in the stomach and, mumbling an apology under my breath, hit the stairs, taking five at a time.

I went out the back way and around to the front and hid in the shrubbery. I didn't wait long. Duval and the others came back in time to find the doorman trying to quiet several of the apartment dwellers. Duval and his men forced the doorman to talk to them, ignoring the others. Then they raced toward the elevator.

They were back down again in less time than I would have thought it would take the elevator to go up and down. Duval left the others at the door. I saw them spread out into the bushes and wait.

I laughed, slipped out from my hiding place and began to track Duval. He was in a big hurry—very big. He was damn near running.

He did just as I thought he would do. He stopped at the first phone booth on the street he came to. He looked around and slipped inside. He had not finished dialing when I opened the door and slipped inside with him. I shoved the .45 in his stomach. *"Bon Soir, Monsieur Duval—de Seraic? It is de Seraic, isn't it, monsieur?"*

He could hardly speak.

"Hello?" The filtered voice coming out of the phone was of no use to me. There was no character to it.

"Tell him you have the bonds." I said. He hesitated. I rammed the gun into his stomach. *"Tell him!"*

"I have the bonds," he said.

"Excellent....bring them to me at once." There was nothing in the voice for me. Who ever it was was speaking through a scrambler.

"Tell him you can't. Tell him what happened to the apartment. Tell him you're afraid you're being followed and the best place would be to meet at the rendezvous near Cuneo."

Duval seemed to be shrinking before my eyes. He grew pale. Then he began to shake. I held the mouthpiece covered with my free hand. I threw my weight against him, shoving him to the back of the booth. *"Tell him!"*

"Monsieur—" he began, looking at me. He repeated everything I had said to him. The other party hesitated.

"...why so far, Duval?"

"Tell him you need time to be sure you are not being followed," I said. He repeated what I had told him.

"... sometimes I think you are too cautious, monsieur. Bon! I will see you near Cuneo. When?"

"At dawn, day after tomorrow," I said to Duval.

He repeated the message. "Tell him everything is under control, everything is all right, but you think it wise to play it safe and give yourself plenty of time."

Duval repeated the final message.

"Perhaps you are right. *Bon!* Cuneo at dawn, day after tomorrow." The line went dead.

Duval hung up the receiver and turned to me. "Empty your pockets," I said.

He began to grow into an old man before my eyes. He emptied his pockets onto the small shelf under the phone. I scooped all of it up and shoved it into my pocket. One of the papers was the neatly folded Swiss bond that I had left for him to find.

"What are you going to do?" His voice was thin and reedy.

"Have you ever seen the Seine at midnight, monsieur?"

He shivered. He said nothing. I called a cab and we got in. "St. Cloud," I said to the driver.

We rode in silence the whole way through Paris and got out before the park. The cab drove off, leaving us alone in the small Paris suburb. We walked to the river and along the banks. There were bushes.

"Strip." I said.

Dutifully he began taking off his clothes. When he was nude, I ordered him to the water's edge. "I am an American agent, de Seraic, and I have your leaders in a trap. By dawn, day after tomorrow, I'll have two dozen men surrounding the rendezvous at the mountain cottage near Cuneo. In forty-eight hours after that I'll have every medallion carrier in Europe."

"There are legions of us—"

"Then we'll just have to build bigger jails."

"Monsieur—" he dropped to his knees— "I beg of you, monsieur. Please. I am an old man." He began to shiver. His white flesh was stark and ugly in the night. Behind him the waters of the river flowed past silently.

At that moment, more than any other single moment in my life I knew the difference between the American culture and the European.

I had to give him his chance.

"Can you swim?"

"No—no, monsieur."

"That is the only thing I can do," I said. "Get in the water."

"Please—no—"

"Into the water. I can't shoot you down, de Seraic. And there is nothing else I can do for you."

He was still on his knees. "Monsieur—there is something I can tell you."

"What is it?"

"My life, monsieur."

"What is it?"

"My life. You must promise me my life!" He screamed.

I didn't want to kill him although he deserved it. There would be no mercy for me. I knew this, yet there was the subtle difference.

"Your life," I said. I threw him his clothes.

We walked back to the center of St. Cloud and stopped at the first café we came to. I poured brandy into him and watched the color come back into his face.

"I cannot tell you anything, monsieur," the old man said—the old man who had aged ten years before my eyes in the last hour—about the Sociéte de la Banderole d'Sang. I—you must believe me, monsieur."

I said nothing.

"I was sent here from Prague on orders. I was given the name of the man and told to rent an apartment in the building that you visited tonight. I was given the name Duval. That is all I know. I waited for three months without leaving the apartment, and then he called. He gave me orders to take care of a mission. He is called Zurrapa—"

"What mission?"

"It was a political assassination in Italy. With the mission I was given the name of a hundred medallion carriers. And I was told of the rendezvous near Cuneo."

"Who was murdered?"

He mentioned the name of an anti-communist labor leader in Milan. I nodded for him to continue.

"That is all I know, monsieur. I operated from Paris and Cuneo." He nodded. "*Oui.* He would call and tell me what he wanted done. And once I failed. Four of those closest to me were found dead."

"How long ago was this?"

"What?"

"The murder of the four?"

"*Oui,* it was four. About a year ago."

"What about Helga de Loon?"

"She was nothing more than a carrier who took orders."

"What about Paul Austin?"

"Who, monsieur?"

"Paul Austin," I said, "a friend of Helga de Loon."

I could not believe that he would try and hold anything back on me at that moment. I had broken his will. He knew it. There was nothing left.

"I'm sorry, monsieur. I don't know that name."

"Paul Austin—I'm sure he was connected to Helga in some way. We suspect him of being a double agent—"

He shook his head. "It means nothing to me."

He took orders from Zurrapa. He had a hundred—sometimes a hundred and fifty and one time as many as two hundred agents—working under him. They worked in groups of ten—fifteen—twenty. They moved freely back and forth from east to west in Europe. There were half a dozen rendezvous places such as the one near Cuneo all over Europe, but he did not know where they were. They operated from half a dozen headquarter groups like that of Duval's. There was only one head, as far as he knew, and that was Zurrapa. They had nothing whatsoever to do with the local Communist Parties. They were independent of all inspection. They were dedicated. They had taken the oath. Once inside there was no way out—except death.

"You mentioned two things that I should know," I said.

"*Oui.* One is the way into the rendezvous in Italy. You would never get in without this information. You would never find it."

"I would find it."

He shook his head. "You are a great agent, monsieur. You did something spectacular in Madrid—but even you would never get into the rendezvous without my help."

"I did something more spectacular than holding up a bank in Madrid, de Seraic."

"What?"

"I'm breaking your organization apart."

His eyes showed his shock. He looked at me with amazement. It was as if there would be something to put me out of the way, something that would stop me. It couldn't be the end. I had seen the same look on the faces of the SS men during the war. And they learned afterwards that it was the end.

"How do I get in?"

He explained in detail how the only pass into the cottage was wide enough for only one man and that it was guarded by a dozen machine guns crisscrossing the approach. There were enough supplies and ammunition in the area to hold off a small army for months. Nothing short of bombing would break through.

"That can be arranged," I said. "What is the second thing?"

"The second thing?"

"Your life, monsieur!" I said harshly, "You said there were two things that I should know."

His eyes were vague. "I don't remember."

I slapped him. He began to cry. "Monsieur. I do not remember!"

I slapped him again. "Think!"

The people in the café were beginning to turn and stare at us. I paid the bill and pulled him into the street. I caught a cab and pulled him in after me. "Café Alié, Malakoff." I said to the driver.

He remembered the second thing when he stopped crying.

"It is the woman, Maria." He said.

I stiffened. I closed my eyes. The memory of her that last moment when I had kissed her sleeping face jarred me to my toenails. "What about her?" I asked in a voice that I did not recognize as my own.

"She has returned to the Cuneo rendezvous. She confided in Anton that she loved you."

"And Anton told you?"

"*Oui.*"

"She is there—at the rendezvous in Cuneo—now?"

"*Oui.* She is waiting for another mission."

We rode a long time, neither of us speaking. The cab stopped for a red light. The traffic poured across before us.

I remembered something. "How was it that I was chosen for the job in Madrid?"

He moved so suddenly that I did not have a chance of grabbing him. He was out of the cab, running directly into the traffic.

I saw him jerk crazily as the truck hit him. It threw him into the air. When he came down he fell in the path of another truck. That one rolled over him.

I was out of the cab as the driver began to scream. I walked slowly through the line of waiting cars in back of me and then dodged off into the nearest alley. I moved fast, running for several block and coming out well away from the place where de Seraic had decided to call it quits.

I caught the Metro and rode into the heart of Paris, caught another cab and returned to Café Alié.

"I have them all," André said, greeting me. "The first twelve I asked knew twelve others. You can leave in two hours if you wish."

I nodded. "*Merci, mon ami.* Get them. Have them all come here, and I will tell them what is to be expected of them."

"Where are you going?"

"To drink some brandy, monsieur, and think about a mademoiselle whom I can never meet again."

The brandy did not help. After the first glass I knew that it wouldn't help.

I had thirty-eight million Swiss francs—nine and a half million dollars. There was a woman that I loved. There were, I knew, other worlds to live in beside the ones we had chosen for ourselves. There were places we could go and live. There were children we could have. There was a life that we could have together.

But the worlds were already chosen. She was in the rendezvous. I would attack it within thirty-six hours.

A sick world.

"A comment." I said. "An opinion. All my own. It can't be changed or modified now, ever. If it takes *this* away from me, then it is a sick world."

It was not long before the first of the men began to arrive. They remained in the café until André rose from his place and closed the doors. He turned out the lights. They came into the small back room and stood around me.

Some of them were old. Some of them had the craggy lines of endurance written on their faces. Most of them were dirty and sweaty. A few wore the clean white shirt and the neatly pressed suit of the office worker or the technician, but most of them worked with their hands.

Everyone had won his honor in the underground. They were twelve to fifteen years older than I. It made little difference that I could see. They were there for one reason and one reason alone. To hear what a man had to say about a threat to France.

Interested in only one thing—France.

Just France.

Chapter Sixteen

ALL OF THEM had read or heard of the bank incident in Madrid. They listened to my story of the criminal-political conspiracy in stony silence. These were not men to dally with. They wanted proof. André spoke up. "Let me hold the bonds, *mon ami*."

"André is a man we all trust," I said. "Agreed?"

They said nothing. They listened and watched.

"André holds the bonds," I said. "At the end of three days, monsieur," I continued, turning to the café owner, "if you have not heard from me—us—take the bonds to the *Sureté* and tell them everything."

I turned to the others and pulled out the bonds. They watched me with the same flinty expression that demands proof and says nothing, does not commit itself until there is proof. I handed the bonds over to the rotund André. "Done," I said.

"What did you say the bonds are worth, monsieur?" A voice asked in the background.

"Nine and a half million dollars in American money. No questions asked. You notice there are no signatures and places for the names of the owners. Upon call, these bonds would be returned to the issuing company for cash payment, plus interest. Whoever holds the bonds gets the money."

One of the better-dressed workers asked to examine the bonds. He looked at them and nodded to the others. "It is true." He said. He turned to me. "Monsieur, anyone who can treat so much fortune so lightly must be telling the truth. I am with you."

Every man in the room voiced his agreement.

"*Bon!*" And for the second time since leaving London on that cold autumnal day I relaxed, remembering sharply that the only other time had been in the rooms of the Hotel Granada. But this was a different kind of relaxation. This was the feeling of being with someone who would help me—instead of trying to stop me.

"How many guns are there among you?"

Every man had a gun and spare ammunition. Nearly all of them were Lugers taken from SS officers slain by the men who now held them. It was a badge of honor.

"We leave at once—but first, how many of you have papers to travel across the Italian border?"

Four of them had papers that would permit them to move freely back and forth between the two countries. "Meet us at the railroad station in Cuneo at six tonight," I said. "You had better leave at once. Whatever money you spend will be refunded to you."

As the four started to leave I stopped them once more. "Choose a leader among you. I will not appoint anyone." There was immediate reaction to this. One of the four who held papers, a medium-height man who looked about forty-five, was tapped. His name was Bassy.

"At six. The station at Cuneo," Bassy said. I nodded.

They left. I turned to the others. "We will leave in two groups. Choose a leader for the second group." There was no question or hesitation for whom they wanted. A tall, hard-looking, wiry man about fifty, with iron-gray hair and wearing a blue smock, stepped forward. He had deep lines running all over his face. "Jacques Maur," he said.

"Take half of the men and go by train to Lyon and then on to Grenoble. I will meet you with a truck on the Modane road at four o'clock in the morning. The others will come with me."

Maur selected his group and left the café through the back door. There were no farewells. They had listened to my story and believed me. They had elected to go along with me. Whatever the outcome, they had offered themselves, their guns, and their knowledge of how to fight to my service and command in the simple dedication to France.

"I need a truck," I said to the group. "One large enough to transport twenty men."

André spoke to one of the oldest in the group. He looked to be a man of sixty.

"He will get the truck," André said as the man hurried from the café. "It will take a little time, but he will get the truck. Just the size you need."

"How long?"

André shrugged his shoulders. "Twenty minutes?"

I laughed. "That will do nicely."

"How will we cross the border, monsieur?" one of the men asked.

"There is a goatherds' pass five miles south of the Mount Cenis railroad tunnel. We cross there. Once in Italy, we will split up and make our way individually to Cuneo. From there we will move into the rendezvous area of the medallion carriers."

"At night, eh?" André said. *"Bon!"*

He took the thirty-eight certificates and shoved them casually into his pocket.

"Now, I give the lie that money does not burn a hole in one's pocket," one of the group said. "Or André would have surely gone up in flame by now!"

The men roared with laughter. Wine was brought out and we fell into talking of the war. It struck me as being just a little corny that these men had turned out so readily to risk their lives again. Not once had the question arose of why I hadn't gone to the police—or, if I was personally in danger, why I hadn't given the information to the police without identifying myself.

They were men who had learned the simple expression of freedom the hard way. The hard way is the school of hard knocks. The hard way is the way that teaches, and the lesson never has to be taught again.

In less than twenty minutes the exhaust of the truck was heard in the back room of the café. We shook hands with André and the men started to climb into the back.

I hung back and spoke to André for a moment. "Should I not return, monsieur," I said, "And it is necessary for you to go to the *Sureté*, there is one other that you might tell all of this to."

"And who is that, *mon ami?"*

"The visiting Americans who come to inquire about me."

"Ahhh-bon! But you will tell them yourself— you shall tell them yourself."

"We shall see, *mon ami*," I said. *"Merci."*

I climbed into the cab of the truck. We rolled off, skirting Paris and moving southward at an angle after passing Villeneuve and avoiding the traffic of Melun. There was no talk. There was nothing to say.

At four in the morning we passed through Grenoble and began picking up the members of Maur's group. It was still dark when we abandoned the truck, which would be picked up later, and searched the vanishing darkness for signs of the goatherds' trail through the rugged mountains of the lower Pennine Alps.

We had been lucky so far. Maur's group had gotten an early train and there was no wait for them along the Modane road. We crossed the border into Italy before dawn and then split into groups of two and three. We began making our way southward towards Cuneo. Maur and another man named Chimné were with me.

I arrived at four in the afternoon. Bassy was alone. "The others are in the café across the square."

I looked across the square where Estuardo had broken away from Maria and myself. "They see us," Bassy said. "Shall I signal them to come or remain?"

"Tell them to wait a short while, then go out of the city, along the old road that extends beyond the fortress walls. There is only one road. They cannot miss it."

"Bon."

"You remain here and direct the others as they come in. Come yourself when the last man arrives. Stay as long as is necessary for all of them to get here. Some may have had to walk the full way."

He nodded and retired to the waiting room of the station—a dignified gentleman waiting for a train and reading his paper.

Maur and Chimné walked slowly out of the station. Presently, out of the corner of my eye I saw the three from the café let themselves out and begin a slow walk after us.

It was dark by the time we had gained the edge of the city and were near the village I remembered seeing when Estuardo and Maria had led me out of the rendezvous—what seemed like ages ago.

We moved into the thick brush and huddled on the ground—waiting, silent, without cigarettes and fighting the increasing cold.

One by one and by twos and threes the men walked along the road and were signaled by Maur. It was nearly ten o'clock before Bassy arrived with the last three of the men. They had walked the entire distance, nearly sixty miles, in fourteen hours. They sank to the ground, exhausted.

I called them around me. "There is one thing to be decided. And that is this. There is a narrow pass leading into the rendezvous—so small that only one man at a time can squeeze through. I've been through the passage and it is very long, about three hundred yards, and approaching it from the outside, it is all uphill climb. There are a dozen machine guns crisscrossing the pass."

No one said a word.

"Before we can attack, we must get through the pass. Also, we need the machine guns to assist in the main assault on the rendezvous area that is further up the hill."

"Do you know where the pass is located, monsieur?" Bassy asked me.

"*Oui.* I can show you the entrance."

"What has to be decided, monsieur?" Maur asked heavily.

"Some of us will have to go ahead and put the machine guns out of commission. And it must be done silently, without guns, for to fire one shot would warn all the others. I do not know if there is an *escape* route out of the rendezvous area. Perhaps the pass I speak of is the only entrance and exit. In such case it would mean little that we fired a gun and warned them, except that they could then prepare themselves. And there is much ammunition and supplies in the area."

"Then the machine guns must be silenced quietly." Maur said.

"*Oui.*"

"Chimné! Claude! Jean! Pétro!"

The four men came to the center of the group. "Did you hear?" Old Maur asked them.

"*Oui.*"

"Follow him," Maur said nodding toward me. "They will see to it that the passage is clear, monsieur."

"Do you have knives?" I asked doubtfully.

"We do not need knives, monsieur," said the one called Pétro. He showed me a four-foot length of wire. He made a loop. "Around the neck," he said.

136

I shuddered. "This way," I said. "How long will it take you?"

"It should be done in the dark, monsieur." Chimné replied.

"Then an hour before dawn, move the others down the road until you see me or one of us," I said to Bassy and Maur.

I stopped. My blood ran cold. "Messieurs, I have made a terrible mistake."

"*Comment.*" Maur's voice was edgy. "What sort of mistake, monsieur?"

"There *is* another way into the rendezvous!"

"How do you know?"

"I was there, as you remember I told you— and while I was there, an automobile arrived and departed. There must be a road!"

"Then your Duval-de Seraic lied to you," Bassy said.

"It must be so."

"But to find the road—" Maur commented.

"It will be easier than trying to silence a dozen machine guns," Bassy said. "Yours is not a mistake, monsieur. It is a blessing."

"Wait!" I cried. "We will find the road! And then we will attack the pass and the machine guns. The others will leave over the road and we will be waiting for them."

"*Bon!*" Maur said.

"How do we find the road?" Claude asked.

"We search for it, *mon ami,*" I said. "Now! Everyone. We spread out over these hills and we find the road!"

I glanced at my watch. It was quarter to eleven. "We have six hours, messieurs. And one hundred square miles." I looked at them. "We will find it," I said. "Return here by five A.M."

"We go!" Maur said to the others.

I started off at the head of them, Maur and Bassy behind me. The others began leaving the road and spreading out into the countryside. In three minutes Maur, Bassy and myself were alone and moving fast in a great circle that I hoped would bring me to the north side of the machine-gun pass—where there might be a road.

***

We made little noise. And we heard nothing. There was no sound from the others. The countryside was as silent as the great stars that hung over our heads. The night was bright, hard and clear.

But there was no hidden road. We returned to the hiding place. By five-ten the first indications of dawn were coming up over the eastern rim of the mountains. By five-ten all of the men had returned. There had been many roads, they reported, but they all led to farms and onto other roads that led in turn to the main roads of the surrounding countryside. There was no road leading into the mountains themselves.

At five-fifteen I spoke to them. "Messieurs, there seems to be no other way, but to go into the pass. But that seems useless and would be a terrible cost to pay—knowing that they would escape through the road we could not find. I do not care about any but the leader—who would know everything about the society. And I know he will be there at dawn—is probably there right now. I cannot ask you to risk your lives on anything as doubtful as our gaining the inner rendezvous only to find the important ones have escaped. I cannot—"

"Monsieur—pardon—but look!" Maur was pointing. I turned. In the half light, I was not sure, but then I *was* sure.

You cannot work with a dog as long as I did, as closely as I did, without knowing it as you would know a person. It was Koko.

I signaled them to be quiet. I stepped out onto the road and into the open. There was no one with her. I waited a full minute to be sure that Rouge was not around and that Koko was alone. Then just before she was too far away to signal, I called her.

She stopped, turned, shot her ears up and came up on her toes. She did not recognize me from the great distance, but she was on the attack.

She stretched out. She traveled at fantastic speed. The men behind me were full of comments about her as she raced toward me.

She recognized me a hundred feet away. It seemed that she put on an added burst of speed to reach me. She skidded to a stop and began to jump into the air and lick at my hand. She barked excitedly, then rolled over on her back for me to rub her stomach.

Finally she calmed down, sat at my side and licked my hand. The men began to move out of the woods. Some of them remembered the stories of the man who had robbed the bank in Madrid with the aid of a well-trained dog.

138

"We will find the road now, messieurs," I said. I took several belts from them and made a leash. I slipped it over her head.

She immediately went into position for guiding me as though I were blind.

The men were amazed.

"Find Maria," I said to the dog. "Take me to Maria!"

She barked, she lunged around.

"Maria! Koko—take me to Maria," I said.

She started off down the road. The men trailed out after me. A half mile down the road, she turned sharply to the left and entered the bushy underbrush.

I saw the secret road instantly. The others saw it too.

It was a watercourse with a bed of small rocks—a twisting and tortured trail around giant trees and rock formations, but was there enough room for a small car to pass.

The tire marks on the face of the rocks on the bed of the now dry stream answered that for us.

I stooped and let the dog go. "Maria!" I said. She raced up the watercourse with excited speed.

In more ways than one I was sorry that I had seen Koko. I did not want to kill any more, and now that we had found the passage out of their rendezvous, there would be bloodshed.

Rouge—and Koko—would protect Maria.

And now I knew she was there—in the gamekeeper's cottage. I had hoped silently throughout the night she would not be there.

"Monsieur Maur. Will you send four men to attack the pass at—" I looked at my watch— "Six o'clock?"

He nodded. The same four he had intended sending in the beginning trotted off without another word.

Hard, cold, silent men.

I started up the watercourse slowly, each step taking me closer to the delicately beautiful woman whose slim body I had known and whose life had become so twisted.

But no more twisted than my own. Rationalize it, Nash, I thought. Does it matter that you are the hunter and are after the kill, that you have right on your side?

No answers to that one. That was a big one that would take years of living before it could be answered. Success that morning would not answer it. It would help. But it would not tell me all. . . .

Quick, Nash, boy, the answer! What did you think about?

Death? Maybe.

We were three quarters the way up the watercourse. I called a halt. We grouped for final instructions.

Chapter Seventeen

THERE WAS THE QUESTION of whether Duval had told the truth about the machine-gun-covered pass.

At six our men began firing from the pass. Short, sniping shots. It was answered immediately by the heavy rattle of emplaced thirty-caliber machine guns. Duval had told the truth.

Five minutes later we heard movement above our position, which was on both sides of the watercourse and strung out for three hundred yards toward the lower road.

We waited. No one was to fire until I gave the signal. I wanted the car to come down. I wanted whoever was in it—alive.

Three men came down, running hard. To my right one of the Frenchmen raised his gun. I waved him back. Two more came down the watercourse.

Then I heard the whine of a car in first gear—straining, bucking against the rocks. The car emerged from around a boulder and was followed by a dozen men. All of them were running.

There was no sign of Maria. Nor of the dogs.

The car was fifty feet away from me. I waved to the others. I stood and showed myself, firing a shot into the air. "Stop!"

The men skidded to a stop and looked around wildly. The men along the watercourse showed themselves.

Those below were trapped.

"Throw down your guns!" I shouted.

Suddenly there was a strange silence that seemed like it was an even louder noise.

I realized then that the machine guns had stopped their commanding chatter.

The men in the watercourse had thrown their hands up and dropped their guns to the ground. The car did not stop. It flashed beneath me.

"Don't shoot!" I screamed to the others. I had seen something inside the car that froze my blood.

But I was too late. There was a burst of a dozen shots from as many guns. The tires blew. The car jerked sideways and rammed into a tree.

I leaped down from the side of the roadway, raced to the car and jerked the door open.

Maria was slumped over the steering wheel, blood covering her chest. She was still alive. She smiled at me and closed her eyes.

Koko and Rouge were both dead. Their furry black bodies lay in a heap on the floor in back.

It ended there for me. There was the last hope. There, dead before me, without life, without breath. Somewhere in the back of my head I had hoped, prayed that something—perhaps even my own change of mind—would make it come into reality.

Now there was only the sickening, cloying feeling of being gutted by a dull knife.

***

Maur had sent one of the men for the Italian police and had searched our captives. They sat now, cowed, sullen, tied, a little afraid of the men who stood over them with guns in their hands and the hard eyed look of the executioner in their eyes.

Somehow they learned that their captors were of the French underground.

I walked among the men sitting on the ground. I saw Anton to one side, staring at the little car. Maria had been removed and placed under a blanket. The dogs were laying side by side, a short distance from her.

"Anton."

He looked up and for a moment I didn't think he recognized me. Gradually his eyes cleared. We looked at each other.

"I would give anything to have prevented it," I said.

"I believe you." He said.

"Did she tell you about me?"

"Only that she loved you, monsieur."

"Did she say that I loved her?"

"*Oui*. She said that you—did—" He stopped and fought back the tears— "That was a good thing when you left her. You did not use her."

"No. I didn't."

"What else is there to say?"

"I need information, Anton. Are you going to give it to me?"

"No, monsieur. Let the others talk. I believed what I was doing was the right thing. Her father believed—"

"And Estuardo?"

"A thief." He spat on the ground.

I nodded. "I can't argue with a man who has fought—well—and lost. I argue with what you fought for."

"I know you do, monsieur."

"Would you like to bury her?"

"*Oui.*" He looked up at me, his eyes pleading.

"I will help you," I said.

Then it came over me. It swept up inside of me like a huge wave from a warm, washing sea. I wept.

I could hardly dig into the winter-frozen ground. It took us three hours of hard, steady progress.

The Frenchmen and the others on the ground watched in silence— the Frenchmen knowing only that I was burying the one I had loved, the others knowing that I was burying Maria—whom they had all known and had loved, too, but in another way.

We buried Koko and Rouge beside her.

Anton, Bassy, Maur and I walked up to the cottage. There were forged passports from fourteen different countries, a hundred-thousand dollars in currency from as many countries to go with the passports. There were maps and photos of banks, bridges, power plants, heavy industrial sites, railyards, rail bridges, naval yards in both Italy and France, and details on how these could be blown up or plundered. But there was no master list of names that would surely be with the leader, unless he had destroyed them and was now posing as a medallion carrier with the others. But I did not think that was likely.

I had enough documented proof of the huge organization and its operations to hand this group over to the Italian police and have them convicted without question.

Anton watched us, smoking, silent. I spoke to him. "Which is the leader?"

He didn't reply or look at me.

"Whoever he was, Anton, he murdered her," I said, coldly, using anything I could to make him talk. "He sent her down in the car to throw us off and give himself time to slip away, isn't that so?"

He stirred, remained silent.

"Anton—"

"You want him because he is the leader of the medallion society!" He said sharply. "I will get him because he murdered her—"

"Let me get him, Anton," I said. "I loved her too."

"No. You would destroy the organization—I only want him."

"I want him just as badly as you do."

"No. You will never find him. He could be in America by now—"

"Is he an American?" I snapped.

He turned away from me. Bassy and Maur were watching and listening. I followed Anton to the window.

"An American—who is he, Anton."

"He is *mine!*" He growled.

"No!" I grabbed him by the front of his shirt. *"Who is he?"*

He was silent.

"He murdered Maria!"

He was silent.

"Tell me!" I shook him.

His eyes met mine. He stared at me hard. He smoked. "Don't you know, monsieur?" He asked with a cynical sneer. "He saved your life the first time you came here—"

"An American who saved my life—"

"I suspected he was not a revolutionary, monsieur," Anton said, his voice full of hate and desire for revenge.

"Who is he?"

"Paul Austin." Anton said simply.

144

The words exploded around my ears like a grenade. It couldn't be Paul. Paul was dead.

"You're lying. Your people killed Paul Austin in Scotland—"

"No, monsieur. He is very much alive—now—this minute."

"Prove it." I found myself ramming a .45 into Anton's stomach. But an old hand like Anton was not going to be intimidated. He smiled.

"I do not have to prove it, monsieur." He shrugged. "But if you want proof—" He turned to the center of the room— "You will have to—find him for yourself!"

He grabbed Bassy's gun and slammed the hard old man up against the wall. To shoot would have been taking a chance on killing Bassy.

"I will get him, monsieur," Anton said. "For both of us."

"No, Anton—wait!"

"There is no need to wait, monsieur. He can only be in one of three places." He smiled. "He was not your friend, Monsieur Nash. He was not my friend. He was nothing but a greedy dog."

He slipped out of the door and ran through the woods. Maur brought up his gun—but I slapped it down.

"No!"

"Why not?" Maur asked.

"I know where he is going," I said. "We will get him alive."

Bassy and Maur looked at me. "How do you know this?"

"He's going after—" I bit hard on my lip— "Paul Austin. I know where to get him."

"But who is Paul Austin—"

"A man—who is supposed to be dead, but who I know now is not dead," I said hollowly.

"How do you know where this one will go?"

"Anton said he would be in one of three places. Why those particular three places?"

They looked at me.

"Three places where the bonds would be, messieurs, nearly ten million dollars in bonds—"

"But the three places?" Maur demanded.

"Can you handle everything here when the police come?" I asked.

"There will be no trouble, monsieur." Bassy said. He stepped to my side. "Go, if you must."

I took one of the forged passports and some of the money. We walked down the watercourse through the men to the road. As we passed the grave, I stopped.

"They tell me she was the most beautiful woman in the world, monsieur."

"In the world," I heard myself saying.

"Everything will be taken care of here," Maur assured me. They walked away. I was left alone at the grave.

***

I returned to Cuneo alone. I was passed on the way by several squads of police and a troop carrier full of soldiers. I stepped into the brush and let them pass. I caught a train to Torino and used the forged passport to catch a plane for Paris.

I was in Paris by seven that evening. I had not slept for nearly forty-eight hours and I was closer to being dead on my feet than I had been in a long time.

Three places where he would be. Where the bonds would be. Duval's apartment would be the first, and finding it looted, he would go to his own place and wait for Duval to show up. But after realizing that Duval was not going to show up, he would start thinking. And when he started thinking, he would remember that the rendezvous had been raided by civilians—French civilians who knew how to handle themselves. And where would the most likely place be for me to get such help?

Paul Austin would figure it that way and he would go straight to André.

I only hoped that Anton would be slow in getting to Paris.

I thought of Maria and then quickly put her out of my mind. It would be longer—perhaps a lifetime would not be enough to take her away from my thoughts completely—but for the moment, I had to put her beautiful face behind me.

Chapter Eighteen

I WAITED UNTIL the lights were out and the front door locked. It had been a long cold wait and the small bottle of brandy was worth every franc I had paid for it.

At two, after the café had been closed for a half hour and I was beginning to think that I might have slipped up, I saw the lights of a cab swing around the corner and pull to a stop a few doors away from the café. Someone walked to the door and tried it, glanced up and down the street, and then slipped around to the back.

I went around the corner and headed for the café. By the time I got around to the back and looked in the window, Paul was checking the bonds and André was standing against the back wall, his hands high above his head. I yanked the .45 and stepped through the doorway.

"Hello Paul," I said.

He went for his shoulder holster.

"Don't try it! I'll kill you where you stand!"

He lowered his hands to the table. André came forward quickly and took the gun out of Paul's coat. "Search him," I said to André. "He used to carry two guns."

Paul looked the same. There was absolutely no change in him. He might have dropped a few pounds, but the same broad, all-American grin was there, the cocky forward tilt of his wide, capable shoulders. His male good looks.

"Hello, Monty. Long time no see."

"Empty his pockets, André." The fat café owner had stepped back, empty-handed. There had been no second gun. "Everything on the table," I said.

The bonds, a thick sheaf of papers, wallet, pen, knife, fountain pen, handkerchief, cigarettes all went on the table. André stepped back.

"The list of names," I said to André. He handed it to me. I glanced through them. It was complete. Thousands of names and addresses — Anton, Estuardo, Duval, José...Maria. I folded the paper and shoved it into my pocket. "Now the bonds," I said.

André made one more trip from the table to my outstretched hand. I shoved them into my pocket, stooped and picked up Paul's gun. "Now call the *Sureté*, André."

"He can't, Monty. I snatched the phone out so he couldn't holler after I left."

I looked at André.

He nodded. "It's true, *mon ami*."

"Then we'll walk," I said. "Let's go, Paul."

"How did you get so wise?" Paul asked. His smile was fading fast.

"I guess I began to suspect a long time ago, but I didn't know it myself."

He looked at me blankly.

"That first night in the rendezvous near Cuneo, Duval and the others were ready to let me have one in the back of the head, but you stopped them. I think I began to suspect when I woke up, surprised to find that I wasn't dead, and that I wasn't even tied. There wasn't one good reason I could give myself for being alive.

"Then later, after the questioning, I heard you drive up in the car. I didn't know who you were at the time, but after talking to you Duval and the others came in and said I was okay—and gave me an elaborate plan for heisting the bank in Madrid." I paused. "By the way, how did you know the bonds would be there, and about Benedicto?"

"One of many sources of information." He answered. He stared at the gun. He was waiting for a chance. Just a thin, reckless chance.

"I think I began to know about that time, but I still couldn't put you with it," I said. "There was a reason."

"Maria," he said.

I felt the pressure tightening on my forefinger. "Yes, Maria. And don't tempt me Paul. I loved her. Don't crap up a situation that could only cause you to get very dead very quickly."

He swallowed hard. He grinned and shrugged it off. "She was a beautiful girl."

"Was!" I said, taking a step forward. "How did you know! You left before they came down the hill—"

He nodded.

"I get it." I said slowly, feeling the words come out like hot marbles, one at a time. "You jammed the feed on the car and probably cut the brake cables too—"

André was as still as stone, listening to us.

"Why—" I shouted, "When you knew we would shoot her full of holes."

"She was going to tell you everything."

I closed my eyes. The shock began to take its full effect. "Why—why—didn't you just shoot her?"

I stared at him.

"I know why! You needed extra time to get away."

I fired—and at the last split second I regained my reason. I pulled the gun sideways with a twist of my wrist.

It was the most difficult thing I've ever done in my life.

And Paul jumped me.

He had the gun wrenched out of my hand before I knew what had happened. He backed up one step, grinning. And then André made a dive for his hand.

"André—no!" I shouted.

It was too late. Paul half turned, fired and never stopped grinning as the heavy slug slammed into André's chest and threw him clear across the room.

I leaped, wildly, kicked hard and managed a glancing blow on his wrist. The gun sailed across the room. We both dove for it.

I reached it first, rolled over to avoid his dive and jammed the gun into his face. "No, I'm not going to kill you, Paul," I said, half crying, half laughing. "You're going to fry!"

I backed him up slowly, moving one arm, then a leg and then another arm until I was upright.

He was still a good man. He had waited until I was in my best position, knowing that I would ease up a little when I thought I was in command again. He came up under the gun hand and caught my wrist.

We went down.

He had always been as strong as a bull and now he proved it. He tightened his grip on my wrist. Our faces were inches apart. He began to grin at me. He knew he was going to win.

I pulled my leg up sharply, aiming for his groin, but he knew I was going to try it and deflected the blow with a twist of his body.

My hand was gradually becoming numb. I tried to wrench free, forgetting about the gun, hoping that I could roll free and get in something that would stun him for a moment.

The pain was getting almost more than I could stand. He continued to grin at me. The gun fell out of my fingers.

He threw me back and picked up the gun.

"Sorry, Monty," he said. And there was no smile on his face now. "Give me the bonds and the list of names."

I did not move. I lay on the floor unable to keep from grimacing with pain from the shooting, needle-like jabs in my arm.

"Get up!"

I rolled over and got to my knees. I sagged into a chair.

He stood on the other side of the room and knelt down to examine André. "Dead," he said to me. Then he grinned. It was completely disarming. It was like a pursuit, when there would be nothing but death facing us and he would turn suddenly and give me that grin.

"The bonds and the names, Monty," he said. He was breathing heavily.

"I should have killed you," I said tonelessly.

"I know that—and you know it." He said. "Now you know what I have to do."

"You'll have to kill me to take the stuff, *mon ami.*"

"Don't make me do that, Monty."

"You'll have to."

He stepped to my side and caught me with a solid left hook.

***

When I came out of it, he was slipping into his coat. He quickly grabbed up the gun and held it on me.

"I'm sorry you woke up, Monty," he said. "Now you'll have to take it with your eyes open."

"What happened, Paul?" I asked. "You owe me that much."

"What do you mean?"

"It started in Antwerp—with Helga. Pick it up from there."

He hesitated. "I haven't got time, Monty. Sorry." He raised the gun "You always did have a problem handling me and my women."

"You owe it to me, Paul!"

"I don't owe anyone anything any more," he said. He slapped his pockets with his hands. "I'm going to be the biggest thief since Hitler, *mon ami*, only I don't want countries and all that jazz—just loot, *mon ami*. Lots of loot."

"You were sleeping with Helga. You were a good agent. You smelled a rat—" I said, leading him on.

He grinned. "It was like taking pie from a baby. Once I got a whiff of what the medallion society was, I went to work. It didn't take much to crack her. I suggested that I become a member—for loot, of course. She was all for that. She was a little weary of the cause. She set up a meet with Duval. I poured in the right answers and made them see how they could spread the society to America. They went for it hook, line and sinker, sweetheart."

He chuckled.

"Then I set up a meet with Duval and a guy who called himself Blanavoa—the meet was to take place in Scotland, and I went on my merry way to fish, if you will remember."

"I remember."

"Turns out that Blanavoa has a strong resemblance to me. We went into the lake regions to fish, leaving Duval back at the Inn. I pumped him dry. I really had them convinced that I was the guy to set up the operation back in the states."

"You weren't a rat at that time, were you?" I asked.

He tightened his lips. "You want to hear this or do I let you have it now?"

"Go ahead, Paul." I said.

"Before I would give him my word about anything, I demanded to know the operation—what would be expected of me. In that way, and from things Helga and Duval had said, I knew this was no penny ante outfit. I could easily add one outfit like he wanted me to set up in the States for every country in Europe—and a few in South America—and come up with a hell of an operation.

"It was the moment he told me that the medallion carriers performed every mission under the penalty of death if they failed or disobeyed—and that they carried out operations such as little bank jobs and jewel robberies to keep them in funds—that the ball stopped bouncing and—I bounced him.

"The luckiest break was his having a complete list of names of every carrier in the world. He was on his way back to eastern Europe after setting up an operation in London when Duval had contacted him. It was my lucky day."

"That's when you made the phone call to me," I said.

He nodded. "I dumped Blanavoa and gave him all my ID stuff. My only hope was that Rex and the lab boys wouldn't get to the body in time to take fingerprints."

"There were many other things," I said, "They could have used. Dental records for one thing."

"It didn't matter at the time," Paul said. "I didn't even bother to go back to the Inn and contact Duval. I went to Glasgow and called him, made a half-assed impersonation of Blanavoa's voice and told him that I had been put in charge of the European division."

"Didn't Duval question this?"

"You forget, boy, this outfit doesn't allow anyone to ask questions. They all know that. That's why they were ready to give you a fast slug in the head in Italy. You asked questions. And besides, I had all the expressions, as we call a password, and I was talking as if I was Blanavoa. Duval didn't see a thing wrong. And then later, when I showed up in Blanavoa's place—" He shrugged— "I had the situation under control. I had other boys I could bring in from any country in Europe to do a job on Duval if he should get out of line."

"But why!" I asked. "You never seemed to be a guy—that would flip—"

"Loot, baby! Loot! Like this in my pocket. Who the hell else can walk around with nearly ten million in bonds in their pocket?"

"I did—"

"Yeah—and you should have taken it and lammed with Maria. No one would have ever known. Rex would have thought you were knocked off somewhere, and the only other person that would have known would have been me. And I would have liked to have seen you two together, sincerely, pal. But it all comes to grief now."

"Not yet, Paul," I said. "What about me?"

"What about you? I suspected that Rex would put out a bloodhound on me—once they figured out that Blanavoa was not Paul Austin—just as a routine check to see if I had defected, which as you must know, is the first thing that entered their heads. I was hoping that I would have covered my trail completely when the nose did show up and either knock them off in an obvious manner, or—" He shrugged again "let it go. I had plenty of protection."

"Back to me." I said.

"Okay, back to you."

"Weren't you curious when you learned that Helga and de Loon were knocked off?"

"Not at all. The Antwerp papers were sure—they're still sure—that it was a robbery motive. You took money and a diamond, didn't you?"

I nodded. "I gave it to Maria," I said.

"I know. That was nice of you."

"Thank you."

"Don't mention it."

"Back to me, Paul," I insisted.

"Can't, Monty. I have to go. Time is running out."

"And the bonds."

He grinned. "And the bonds. They're going to set me up, Monty. I'm going to establish a headquarters with this loot. I'm going to make those stupid bastards pay right through the nose every time they have a single communistic thought."

"Back to me," I said.

"One more question," he said. He wasn't kidding. He was going to let me have it. I didn't know whether I stood a chance on jumping him or not, but as long as I had him talking, I was in a jockeying position. "Shoot."

"Why did you send me out on that mission to Madrid? And how did you know the bonds were there?"

"I thought I answered that one for you?"

"No."

"One of the reasons neither you, nor I, nor any other cop, ever heard of the medallion carriers is that they never pulled a heist on a legitimate bank, jewel house, or what have you. Only on those people that couldn't yell to the cops. I have files on the wealth of every crook in Europe."

"How did you get that?"

"Every one of them banks their loot in Switzerland. We have several very good groups in Switzerland who supply us with the information."

"Then why the Madrid job? That was certainly going to get out to the cops. That would mean cops all over you."

"It was the biggest of the lot. Aside from some of the South American ones. This way I could make enough in one haul to really set things up. And there wasn't one carrier or combination of carriers that would do it. When you showed up, it was a natural. Monty, I said to myself, if there is any one guy in the world that can crack that box in Madrid, it's Monty Nash."

"Then why send Estuardo out to gun me down?"

"Maria told me you had been picked up by Orrick and Sheldon. I was afraid that you were getting close. But you certainly took Estuardo and those other two nicely. I should have sent a dozen boys after you."

"Maria never told you," I said.

"She saw you get into the car with Orrick and Sheldon. She followed you. She saw Sheldon go into a café or drugstore and make a phone call. When he came back, you beat it up an alley. I know those two boys. Orrick is the best judo man in the world and Sheldon hates your guts. You couldn't have gotten away from them if you had wanted to."

"I did. But I won't argue with you. I still don't believe that Maria told you."

"She told me! She's a very dead, no-good communist medallion carrier. I hate to put it to you like this. I would have liked to send you on your way with happy thoughts about her. But you wanted to know. I told you, Monty." He sighed. "She was beautiful, and under any other circumstances, I would have fallen for her myself. But she was rotten like all the rest of them."

"Did you know about the attack on the rendezvous?"

"No."

"Then you expected Duval?" I said.

"Yes." He grinned. "But I saw the attack as a good thing. Let you take some worthless documents and garbage about blowing up bridges and naval yards and maybe it wold take Rex off my back."

"But what about me? You must have known that I'd hang on until I came up with the right answers."

"Had that figured too, Monty." He grinned. "The best way to get a guy like you is legally. The Spanish police are still looking for the guy that pulled the bank job and the one who knocked off Estuardo and his buddies. You would be hunted down like a common crook, Monty. No one would believe you."

"But suppose Duval had lammed out with the bonds?"

He laughed. You don't know this outfit, buddy. They don't do things like that—pain of death for failure in a mission or to disobey, remember?"

He sobered. His face hardened. "So long, pal. Maybe I'll see you again—in hell."

I jumped.

He brought the gun up, but I had already made my move. There was an explosion in my ears, then a sudden flash of lights in my brain.

I fell—only I couldn't find the damn floor. I kept falling and falling and falling—

Then I found it. "Nice floor," I said. "So happy to see you at last..."

155

Chapter Nineteen

ANTON STOOD OVER ME, slapping my face. "Wake up, monsieur!"

I opened my eyes a little more. I raised myself up. He backed across the room holding a gun on me. I turned.

Paul was stretched out on the floor. There was a neat little hole in the back of his head right at the base of the brain. There wasn't much blood.

"Why—did you do it?"

He spat on the floor. "I am a revolutionary, monsieur. I fought in Spain and later at Stalingrad. Maria's father was by my side for all that time. We fought together. I killed Paul Austin because he murdered Maria."

"But you saved my life."

"She loved you. She confided to me that she was going to leave the society and come to you," he said in a voice full of emotion. "I promised her father—I promised, monsieur—on his death bed that I would take care of her and that I would see that she was happy." He stopped and looked at Paul's body. "She was happy with you. She told me of the Hotel Granada, monsieur, and how you left her—"

I waited. He was near tears. He continued. "This dog—" He kicked Paul's body— "made a waste of my life."

"I—don't understand."

"He made me see, monsieur, that all of these years—all of the fighting—all of the plans and the terrible struggle to go on when there seemed no way to go—all of it came to nothing through this dog."

You don't often see a big hard man broken in spirit. I have see it only a few times. It is the most tragic thing one has to endure. Death, while also tragic, is swift, complete, sure. There is no return. But here, Anton, like Duval, was aging before my eyes. The tired old revolutionary who had fought wisely, well, with courage and convictions, saw that it was useless.

Paul was not the reason for his defeat. Just the primer cap that set everything off.

"Nothing, monsieur, will ever replace the greed in men. It will always be with us," he said at last. "Often I have told myself that the way things were going in Poland, Hungary, and elsewhere were the results of capitalistic spies and unrest—but for a long time now I have known the truth. Those who give the orders, monsieur are like this dog at my feet. Greedy men. That will never change." He stepped to the door.

"Wait, Anton!" I said. "Why go away? You know so much—you can—"

"Fight against them now?" He smiled. "Ten years ago, perhaps even five. I would have had enough fire left to change sides. I know the truth. But no more, monsieur. I am an old man. I will go away— perhaps back to Spain—or Italy."

He waved at me. "*Bon soir, mon ami.* Remember, she loved you—and she was coming to you. This one murdered her to protect his greed."

He slipped through the door.

***

I took the papers out of Paul's pocket and grabbed the bonds. Then I heard the shots. I stepped to the door and raced through to the front of the café.

Tris Guardian, Orrick and Sheldon had Anton corned in the alley leading to the back of the café.

There were a few more shots on either side—and then I saw Anton bless himself, kissing a crucifix made of his thumb and forefinger. Then he stepped clear and stood open. He moved away from the alley and out into the open, taking half a dozen steps to the middle of the street.

I thought he was trying to get away. Then he stopped.

He held a Luger in each hand. And both hands were jumping. I saw Sheldon go down—he rolled over and held his shoulder. Then Orrick caught one in the leg. The Lugers were still pumping when Tris got him with two .45's in the head, tearing the whole top of his skull off.

I ran out into the street. Tris came forward to meet me. "You okay, Monty?"

"Yeah—Sheldon and Orrick?" I asked.

"Just wounded."

I looked down at the big man stretched out in the middle of the street in the dark Paris suburb. "It had to be this way—the only way."

"He must have gone nuts," Tris said. "Coming out in the open like that." And then Tris made a gentle movement with his hand. His voice was softer. "Still—he was two down and one to go ..." He paused. "A good man."

"A good man," I said. "They're all good men. There's just one thing wrong."

"What?"

"They never learn that the best way to win is to vote."

"But they got to win the vote first," Tris said.

"Maybe they will someday, Tris, with our help."

"Maybe."

Orrick limped up to our side, followed by a moaning Sheldon.

"Where's Paul?" Tris asked.

"Paul! You know—I mean—"

"We've known since the day you took my gun and beat it out of the Worthington Gardens establishment," he said.

"Then why?" I felt growing outrage. "You *knew* and—you let me—"

"Rex will explain it all to you, Monty," Orrick said through clenched teeth.

"It better be good," I said.

"Where's Paul?"

"Inside. Dead. He killed André."

I turned away and he started walking down the street.

"Hey—where are you going?"

I didn't answer. I began to run. Running might help. Running might drive it out. If I ran fast enough I would run it right out of my system.

I ran—I ran—and I kept running.

Chapter Twenty

LONDON WAS ENJOYING one of its half dozen sunny days during the winter. I rode with Tris out the double drive west and into the Gardens.

Rex greeted me with an outstretched hand. "Welcome back, Monty."

I refused to take his hand. He glanced at Tris. "Hard feelings, Monty?"

"Very hard," I said.

"I'll try to make you see my position," he said. He turned and we followed him into the office. He sat down behind his desk. I still stood.

"Sit down, Monty. You look beat."

"I am beat," I said. "But I'll stand. I may not be staying long."

He pulled on his lip and glanced at Tris.

"Well?" I demanded.

"Monty, we never suspected you for a minute."

"That's a lie," I said. "You thought I was a creep."

"No. I have the records to prove it."

"Your records can be made to read any way you want them to read," I said.

He got mad. He slammed his fist on the desk. "All right! All right! I used you. I would use my own mother if it would have delivered the medallion carriers!"

That made sense when I thought about it, which was not right at the moment. At the moment I wanted to get my hands on him. But I was still weak, and Tris had not left the room. And it didn't look like he was going to.

"Okay," I said. "So I was the pigeon."

"Right!" He said harshly. "None of us are precious around here, and you know that better than anyone else."

I nodded, conceding the point. "Go on."

"We had been suspecting Paul for a long time before you came up with the phone call and the R-map coordinates."

"What about them?" I asked. "Any reason why he used them?"

"You talked to him before he died. Did he give any reason?"

I shook my head. "He was too busy telling me how he was going to become an international crook."

Rex shook his head. "They were phony, of course. Just to throw us off the track."

"How did you suspect Paul?"

"Paul was a damn good agent. And we had damn good information that Helga de Loon was carrying a medallion. If Paul was so close to her—there was damn good reason that he had learned about it. But he hadn't said anything to us."

I nodded. It fit with what Paul had told me.

"When he pulled the phony gag, delivering us a dead man supposed to be himself, and you came in with a lot of jazz about R-map coordinates, there was only one thing to do. That was decided by GloSec Europe before you got here that morning. We never once believed that you knew of Paul's suspected activities. But we also knew that the only man—the *only* man that could find him—was the one man that knew his record and his ways better than the psychologist and his own mother— and that man was you. But we also knew that Fox first squads are like twin brothers. There isn't a twin in the world that would go after his brother—the way we knew Paul had to be pursued. The obvious thing was to make you believe that we suspected you as well—knowing that you would hightail it off across the channel and start in looking for something to clear you both. You knew things that we didn't know. But we knew you wouldn't come up with them—even if you wanted to—because of the twin brother emotion that was involved. We had to press you. We pressed. And you delivered."

He paused and looked at me. "Monty, it was a hard, cruel thing to do. But you've got to see it my way. We got them. Every one of them, and fourteen rendezvous points throughout the world are being mopped up right this minute."

I closed my eyes. Everything he said made sense. I think I knew he would have logical answers for what had happened. But I wasn't ready to accept them. "Okay, Rex. Thanks. I can't shake hands now. I'm still too involved."

"That's okay. As long as you report back after a six-week leave in the States—ready for work."

I shook my head. "I've had it. I couldn't go through another training period with another guy. I'm too old, for one thing. Even then, there was only one guy for me, and he's on a slab in a Paris morgue."

"We don't want you to operate as a Fox head of a first squad. You're to be the trouble shooter. The solo man."

"Alone?"

"Strictly," Rex said. "Go on now. Back to Cleveland and eat some of Mom's home-cooking for a few weeks. See the old gang and tell them about the night life in Paris as a newspaperman. Then come back."

"I can't answer you now. I may not come back." I said, meaning it.

"I'll take that chance." He sipped his cup of coffee and then stood. He came around the desk, and offered me his hand.

I took it.

"The plane tickets will be at your apartment in two hours. With all the back pay and allowances. You had a lot of expenses on this, so we're just giving you an open expense account for this trip."

"By the way, what happened to the bonds?"

He shrugged. "Señor Benedicto is a bum, rat, hood, gangster and white slaver. But they were his. They had to go back, with an explanatory note through diplomatic channels—that will also take care of Estuardo." He coughed. "We made it look like it was—Estuardo."

I said good-by. I rode back to the apartment and packed. I thought of Paul and the phone call that had started it all. Then I forgot him. And I began thinking about Maria.

I wouldn't forget her. Cleveland would not erase that. I called the West End redhead and was informed that she was no longer a Miss—but a Mrs. All things come to an end.

My landlady grumbled about having to wait for her rent so long and demanded three months rent in advance if I was going to remain.

That had not been decided yet. But I knew it had been decided. I paid the rent and told her I would be back in six weeks.

I rose above London in the giant plane and started out over the Atlantic. The world was going mad—it *was* mad. But I knew there were times when it would stop and be still. It nearly always did for lovers. It had stopped, briefly, in a shabby little hotel in Madrid.

Briefly. Then gone on.

Biography

Richard Jessup (01/01/1925 – 10/27/1982) was born in Savannah, Georgia and died in Nokomis, Florida. He lived in and out of orphanages until age sixteen – when he ran away to join the United States Merchant Marine. In eleven years of seamanship, he claimed he read a book a day and learned to write by typing out the complete text of *War and Peace* and editing out the errors – he subsequently threw the edited work in the ocean. Jessup was married to Vera in 1944 and had a daughter named Marina. He left the Merchant Marine in 1948 to become a fulltime author. He was at the typewriter ten hours a day.

His first novel, *The Cunning and the Haunted*, was published in 1954 and filmed as *The Young Don't Cry* in 1957. Three other novels were also adapted to film – *The Deadly Duo*, *Chuka*, and *The Cincinnati Kid*. He sold the movie rights to the 1971 novel *Foxway* but it was never filmed. Jessup published eleven novels – primarily westerns and spy thrillers – as Richard Telfair. His last novel, *Threat*, was published in 1981.

Jessup's obituary claims he wrote under multiple pseudonyms and published over sixty novels. At this time we can only confirm the pseudonym Richard Telfair and the existence of thirty-four published novels.

Bibliography

Written as Richard Jessup
1954 – The Cunning and the Haunted (The Young Don't Cry)
1955 – A Rage to Die
1956 – Cry Passion
1957 – Cheyenne Saturday
1957 – Comanche Vengeance
1958 – Long Ride West
1958 – Lowdown
1958 – Texas Outlaw
1959 – The Deadly Duo
1959 – The Man in Charge
1960 – Sabadilla
1960 – Night Boat to Paris
1961 – Chuka
1961 – Port Angelique
1961 – Wolf Cop
1963 – The Cincinnati Kid
1967 – The Recreation Hall
1969 – Sailor
1970 – A Quiet Voyage Home
1971 – Foxway
1974 – The Hot Blue Sea
1981 – Threat

Written as Richard Telfair
1958 – Day of the Gun
1958 – Wyoming Jones
1959 – The Bloody Medallion
1959 – The Corpse that Talked
1959 – The Secret of Apache Canyon
1959 – Wyoming Jones for Hire
1960 – Scream Bloody Murder
1960 – Sundance
1961 – Good Luck, Sucker
1961 –The Slavers
1962 – Target for Tonight

Film Adaptations
1957 – The Young Don't Cry
1962 – Deadly Duo
1965 – The Cincinnati Kid
1967 - Chuka

Made in the USA
Charleston, SC
08 November 2011